"A few kisses don't count as a sin!"

"I'll be frank," Piers continued. "I want you. There's a gap in your life and I give you fair warning that I intend to fill it." He leaned forward and took hold of Chloe's hand.

Chloe's eyes dropped to hide her sudden rush of excitement at the prospect. "We hardly know each other," she said obliquely.

"A condition I intend to remedy," Piers assured her.

Catherine George was born in Wales and early in life developed a passion for reading, which eventually fueled her compulsion to write. Marriage to an engineer led to nine years in Brazil at a gold-mine site. It was an experience she would later draw on for her books. Now her husband helps manage their household so that Catherine can devote more time to her writing. They have two children—a daughter and a son—who share their mother's love of language and writing.

Books by Catherine George

HARLEQUIN ROMANCE
3129—ARROGANT INTERLOPER
3147—A CIVILISED ARRANGEMENT
3177—UNLIKELY CUPID
3201—BRAZILIAN ENCHANTMENT
3236—LEADER OF THE PACK
3261—OUT OF THE STORM
3310—LAWFUL POSSESSION

HARLEQUIN PRESENTS
1065—TOUCH ME IN THE MORNING
1152—VILLAIN OF THE PIECE
1184—TRUE PARADISE
1225—LOVEKNOT
1255—EVER SINCE EDEN
1321—COME BACK TO ME

EVIDENCE
OF SIN
Catherine George

Harlequin Books

TORONTO • NEW YORK • LONDON
AMSTERDAM • PARIS • SYDNEY • HAMBURG
STOCKHOLM • ATHENS • TOKYO • MILAN
MADRID • WARSAW • BUDAPEST • AUCKLAND

ISBN 0-373-03353-2

EVIDENCE OF SIN

First North American Publication 1995.

Printed in U.S.A.

CHAPTER ONE

SOMEWHERE between the third and fourth toast Chloe suddenly reached the end of her tether. Under cover of cheers and applause for the two happy couples she slipped from the crowded room, managed to reach the hall unnoticed and fled along the passage to the large, warm kitchen. Snatching a coat from the hooks in the back porch, she let herself out of the house and ran through the frosty, starlit garden, careering wildly down the slope of the lawn in her satin shoes. Gasping in the bitterly cold air, she made for the laurel hedge near the stream which divided the Parsonage from the house next door and slid through a gap to collapse on the decrepit bench she always made for in times of stress. Breath tearing painfully through her lungs, she sat slumped, staring into the water splashing its way with such callous cheerfulness over the stones along its bed.

So this was it: end of the line, time to face facts. The man she'd loved for so long was now not only officially engaged to someone else but, as anyone with half an eye could see, was so pleased with the arrangement that he couldn't wait to rush his betrothed to the altar.

Chloe hugged her arms across her chest, reacting to the thought with almost physical pain. No tears, she told herself fiercely. She'd shed far too many on this subject already. She sniffed loudly, swallowing hard on the lump in her throat. It wouldn't be the first time the laurels had hidden her misery from the world. But even as she promised herself it would be the last a violent sob was

5

torn from her, and she was defeated by her own grief. She fought hard for control, but it was some time before a last shuddering sigh signalled the end of the storm.

'Forgive me, but is there some way I could help?' enquired a disembodied male voice.

Chloe froze.

'Don't worry, I can't see you through the leaves,' assured the voice. 'I'm late, so I took the liberty of a short-cut by way of the gate at the bottom of the garden.'

'If you just carry on along the gravel walk you'll arrive at the front door,' croaked Chloe in a hoarse whisper.

'By which I take it you'd like me to get the hell out of here and leave you alone.'

Who on earth was this? thought Chloe wildly.

'I think you should tell me what's wrong,' went on the relentless voice. 'You'll feel better if you get it off your chest. It's a proven fact that it's easier to confide in strangers.'

'Not for me,' hissed Chloe, careless of her manners by this time. 'Go away—I mean, go on in. *Please.*'

'That's better.' Satisfaction coloured the voice.

'Better?'

'You're annoyed now, instead of—desolate.'

His choice of adjective almost started Chloe off again. She clenched her fists, breathing deeply as she fought the tears back.

'Tell me,' commanded the voice. 'Why are you alone and weeping, Niobe, when joy seems unconfined in the house? I can hear the music from here.'

Chloe ground her teeth in angry silence.

'If you won't tell me, perhaps I could make a deduction or two.'

Reminding herself forcibly that the man, whoever he might be, was also a guest, Chloe quelled an urge to tell her unwanted companion exactly what to do with his deductions.

'Let me see... My invitation here tonight was to a party to celebrate a double engagement,' mused the voice. 'The son and daughter of the house and their respective partners, I believe. You could be said daughter, already regretting the arrangement, or just a friend of the family, secretly rent by passion for one of the gentlemen involved.'

This time shock held Chloe speechless. The stranger's shot had found target with uncanny accuracy.

'Ah, well,' drawled her unseen companion, 'I see you're not of a mind to confide. Nevertheless I think your tears have dried, mystery lady. In which case I'll take myself off to make apologies to my hostess. Farewell, Niobe. Your secret's safe with me. My lips are sealed. No one, I swear, shall ever know I heard a tearful maiden languishing behind the laurels.'

Burning with a variety of emotions, Chloe listened, tense, as his footsteps retreated along the gravel walk. She gave herself five minutes longer to pull herself together, then emerged furtively from her hiding place. She looked up at the house, outlined in all its Gothic Victorian eccentricity against the night sky. Lights blazed and music thumped like a giant heartbeat from the open windows on the ground floor. She sighed raggedly, hating the thought of going in. But more time spent outside would probably bring someone in search of her. Which would be a disaster with her face in its present sodden state. She hurried silently up the slope of the lawn to the back of the house, returned her ancient sheepskin to its peg, and flew on tiptoe up the back stairs to her room.

Ten minutes later Chloe strolled down the front staircase, flags flying and retouched eyes bright, every glossy red hair in place, her smile brilliant as she descended towards a group of her mother's friends in the hall below.

'There you are, Chloe!' exclaimed her mother. 'Why aren't you dancing?'

'No one's asked me yet,' returned Chloe gaily, then almost missed a step as her eyes met those of a tall man she'd never seen before. He was slim, with thick fair hair and a hawk-nosed, confident face. And without any effort he was very obviously the focal point of the group smiling up at her.

'Steady the buffs, darling. Come and meet our new neighbour,' said Mrs Lawrence, beaming with pleasure.

The newcomer inclined his head. 'Piers Audley. How do you do?'

Chloe's heart took a nosedive. The voice, which somehow managed to be crisp and drawling simultaneously, was unmistakable. 'Chloe Lawrence,' she said woodenly. 'How—how nice you could come. Welcome to Little Compton.'

Their eyes held for a moment, then Piers Audley smiled.

'I believe the music's changed to something I can cope with. Since by some miracle you lack a partner at the moment, will you be mine?'

His choice of words won him a startled look from dark blue eyes, but his own, heavy-lidded and thick-lashed, were so blandly inscrutable that Chloe inclined her head in reluctant consent. Wishing passionately she'd stayed in her room and bolted the door, she walked ahead of Piers Audley to join the crowd in the shabby, high-ceilinged drawing-room.

The party was in full swing by this time, the speeches over and the furniture pushed back against the walls to make room for dancing. As Chloe and her companion joined the fray the lights were lowered, and guests who minutes before had been throwing themselves around came together in couples, moving slowly to music with a slow, sentimental beat. Over Piers Audley's shoulder Chloe caught a glimpse of Marcus's dark head bent close to the gleaming blonde curls of his Lisa, and in a far corner she could see her sister Jessica making very little pretence of movement at all in the arms of Dr David Warren, her handsome husband elect.

'Are you recovered, Niobe?' murmured Piers Audley, and Chloe sighed, resigned.

'So you knew it was me.'

'It wasn't difficult to work out. Once I discovered there was another daughter of the house, temporarily missing, it seemed odds on she must be the grieving nymph among the laurels.'

Chloe shot a hostile look at the aquiline, clever face. 'Mr Audley——'

'Not so formal, please.'

'Piers, then. Could you *please* forget you heard me making such a fool of myself tonight?'

'If you mean will I never mention it to anyone, that goes without saying. But your woe was heart-rending. I confess to enormous curiosity as to the cause.'

'Remember the cat,' advised Chloe tartly.

'I'm unlikely to die of curiosity.' His eyes held hers. 'Mainly, I warn you, because I intend to have it satisfied. Some time.'

Chloe was saved from out-and-out rudeness by a welcome pause in the music. Lights flicked on, and with relief she introduced her partner to Marcus and Jess and several neighbours eager to meet the new owner of Clieve House. When supper was announced a moment later Piers Audley seemed fully absorbed into a crowd of her mother's contemporaries, Chloe noted with relief, and for the rest of the evening, she promised herself, she'd give the disquieting stranger a wide berth.

'All right, little one?' asked Marcus, as they went into supper, and Chloe laughed, shutting all thought of Piers Audley and tears out of her mind.

'You're the only man in the world who could ever call me "little one"!'

Lisa sighed enviously. 'I just wish I were your height, Chloe. You seem to eat anything you like and still stay slim as a reed. I only look at a bar of chocolate and I gain inches everywhere.'

'Never mind, darling,' said Marcus, dropping a kiss on the gleaming blonde curls. 'Men prefer their women round and cuddly.'

Chloe gave him a wry look. 'Gee, thanks.'

Marcus grinned, unrepentant. 'Come off it, Chlo. You know damn well they fancy tall, lanky redheads too— don't I know it! When your face was plastered over every news-stand in the old days I couldn't move for blokes pestering me for your telephone number.'

'*And* you had a famous photographer for a boy-friend. I don't see how you could bear to give all that up, Chloe,' said Lisa, shaking her head in wonder.

'I'm sure you don't,' said Jess drily, and thrust a plate into Chloe's hand. 'Eat. Gwen's orders.'

'I'll fill it for you,' offered David, his bright blue eyes teasing as he pushed Chloe towards the laden table. 'Come on—you don't have to count calories any more, cover girl.'

'If I'd had to count calories I wouldn't have been one,' retorted Chloe. 'Willpower was never my strong point.'

'So I've heard,' commented Lisa, smiling sweetly. 'Marcus says you had so many men after you at one time it's a wonder his hair isn't grey.'

Marcus gave his betrothed a frown which brought colour to her cheeks. 'Darling, I didn't put it quite like that.'

Jessica put a selection of delicacies on to Chloe's plate. 'Go on, eat. And while you're at it, tell all about the charismatic Mr Audley. Our legal eagle celeb. is younger than I expected—seriously yummy, in fact!' She looked across the room at the elegant man cornered by a brace of local matrons.

'You know as much as me.' Chloe speared a prawn without enthusiasm. 'I've never met him before.'

'You were dancing with him,' said David, mouth full. 'He must have said something.'

'He was—charming,' said Chloe, and smiled up at him. 'Polite enough to dance with me when he found I was a wallflower.'

'Wallflower!' The others hooted in unison, David giving her an affectionate squeeze which attracted a keen look from Piers Audley across the supper table. He smiled very deliberately at Chloe, who, much to the interest of her companions, blushed to the roots of her hair.

'Well, well!' Marcus raised an eyebrow. 'Something tells me our VIP fancies little Chloe. Let's rescue the poor guy. Mrs Dawson is either asking him for a donation to the church restoration fund or bullying him into a talk for the WI.' And, laying his plate on a window-ledge, Marcus strolled away, head and shoulders above everyone in the room.

'Isn't he thoughtful?' sighed Lisa. 'You two are so lucky to have a brother like Marcus.'

Jess exchanged a grin with Chloe. 'We offer up prayers of gratitude for it daily, don't we? But he's no saint, Lisa. He's only human.' She smiled at her fiancé. 'You're human too, darling, aren't you?'

'You can say that again!' David leered suggestively at Chloe. 'I only wish my religion allowed polygamy. Then I could marry both of you.'

Lisa, who had a tendency to take things literally, looked scandalised.

'Stop it!' said Chloe, grinning, then stiffened as she saw Marcus bringing Piers Audley across the room to join them. But as several other guests gravitated towards them at the same time she seized the chance to slip away to join her mother to help serve the puddings.

'Darling, there's no need,' said Gwen Lawrence in an undertone as she ladled syllabub into glass bowls. 'Louise Dawson would give a hand in a minute. You should be with the others.'

'My place is here with you,' said Chloe firmly, and smiled radiantly into the dazzled eyes of two of Marcus's colleagues, both men plainly more interested in Chloe than the array of delicacies she offered.

But however much she busied herself with other guests, to her annoyance she found herself constantly aware of Piers Audley, who, it seemed, had no taste for sweet things. From the corner of her eye she saw David helping him from a vast platter of cheese on the sideboard across the room, and relaxed enough to indulge in a little badinage with some of the medical fraternity invited by Marcus and Jessica to the double celebration.

But once everyone was served Chloe found her way from the dining-room barred by the tall elegant person of Piers Audley, coffee-cup in either hand.

He smiled at her, in a way which told her he knew his was the last company she wanted. 'Your brother suggested I take you into the hall and make you sit down and drink this. I have it on the best authority that you like it sugarless with a dash of cream. May I have the pleasure of your company for a while?'

Knowing she'd risk maternal wrath if she offended the star guest, Chloe gave in gracefully.

'Of course. Thank you.' She led the way from the room into the draughty, stone-flagged hall to an oak settle half hidden from view under the arch of the back stairs. 'Let's sit here, then. Uncomfortable, but a little quieter than anywhere else at the moment.'

'You've been avoiding me,' he drawled, amused. 'It isn't the least necessary, you know. I gave you my word.'

Taken aback at such a frontal attack, Chloe bit her lip, then shrugged, returning his candour. 'Even so, I'm sure you can appreciate my embarrassment. I didn't anticipate an eavesdropper to my—my lapse out there.'

'I swear your secret's safe with me.' A pair of hooded amber eyes held hers. 'And as far as I can see, no one else seems to have the remotest idea that you languish after your sister's fiancé.'

Chloe's heart gave a great thump. 'Why—why should you imagine my tears were for David? I could have been crying about any man here, or even some man who isn't here at all.'

He shook his head. 'I was watching that lively little family tableau from across the room. Your body language told me a great deal. And I'd hazard a guess that Dr Warren is no more immune to you than you to him, despite his alliance with your attractive sister.'

Chloe set her cup down with exquisite care. 'One would think your field was psychiatry rather than law, Mr Audley.'

'I wouldn't be good at my job if I didn't make a study of human nature, Chloe Lawrence.' He smiled down into her eyes.

Her answering smile was brilliant as she saw her chance to change the subject. 'And you're *very* good, by all accounts. Even here in Little Compton your success rate is well known. Is it true that you get your clients off nine times out of ten?'

He shrugged non-committally. 'If you can believe the popular Press. May I fetch you more coffee, or would you like a drink?'

'What I would really like,' said Chloe, with sudden, quiet vehemence, 'is to go to bed, but as the music's starting again I suppose I'll just have to do my bit to entertain the troops.'

'You could always stay here and entertain me instead.'

Chloe sat very still. 'It wouldn't do for me to mon-opolise our guest of honour, Mr Audley.'

'Even if there's nothing I'd like better?' he queried, the hint of amusement very much in evidence in his drawling, assured voice.

'Why?' she demanded, looking him in the eye. 'Not that I need to ask!'

'I'm sure you don't,' he returned, a smile twitching his lips. 'It's perfectly obvious. You're the most dec-orative woman present. Besides, you rouse my curi-osity——'

'That's not what I meant—all you really want is to know why I was crying.'

'That too,' he agreed, his eyes holding hers, 'but if you imagine that's *all* I want you must have far less experience of men than I'd have expected.'

'Expected?' Chloe bristled. 'What do you mean by that?'

'Only that a face and body like yours must be a magnet to my sex.'

She got to her feet abruptly. 'There's more to me than the way I look, Mr Audley.'

He nodded as he stood up. 'You don't have to tell me that, Chloe Lawrence. That's why you interest me. I find your hint of mystery totally irresistible.'

Chloe's mouth tightened. 'Are you always so direct with women on such short acquaintance?'

'Only with those I meet in such fascinating circumstances,' he assured her suavely.

The approach of one of David's friends saved Chloe the necessity of a withering response. 'Thank you for bringing me coffee, Mr Audley,' she said with a saccharine smile. 'Time to return to duties, I think. Will you excuse me?'

'Only with greatest reluctance,' he assured her, an appreciative gleam in his eye as Chloe smiled with radiance at the dazzled man who'd come in search of her.

As she joined the dancing it suddenly occurred to her that her sparring with Piers Audley had been useful in one way, at least. For several minutes at a time she'd actually given no thought to the grief which had sent her running to her hiding place for sanctuary earlier on.

For the rest of the evening Chloe put on a bright, skilled act which made her the central pivot of the party as far as the majority of male guests were concerned. But Piers Audley made no attempt to dance with her again. To her secret chagrin he seemed content with the company of the older Little Compton residents, all of whom were eager to express a warm welcome to the newcomer in their midst. But every now and then Chloe would catch him looking at her with an irritating hint of challenge which spurred her on to play out her role of quintessential party girl to the end. The most irritating—and surprising—thing of all, she discovered, was the fact that all the other men she danced with seemed utterly insipid after her exchange with Piers Audley. While the only man who could have stood comparison with the sophisticated barrister was much too engrossed in his fiancée to have any time for Chloe Lawrence.

As the hour struck midnight the usual pandemonium broke out, with kisses all round to mark the arrival of the New Year. Chloe was passed from hand to hand, the kisses she received varying in degree from brief and affectionate to the more intimate variety which she put an end to as swiftly as possible. When she came to Piers Audley she felt a sudden, unexpected prickle of anticipation, and braced herself in readiness, but he eyed her hectic flush with amusement, and contented himself with a mere shake of the hand.

'May the New Year be happier for you, Chloe Lawrence.'

'Thank you.' She smiled at him, furious with herself for feeling so disappointed. 'Happy New Year to you, too.' Their eyes held for a moment, then with a polite little nod she excused herself to help Marcus and Jess hand out champagne.

Much to Chloe's regret some guests were staying overnight. Not that there was any problem with space. The rambling old house had several attic bedrooms in addition to the others in more normal use, but tonight Chloe could have wished her home were small, without such scope for visitors. She would have given much to speed the last guest on the way, lock the door on the world and take to her bed for the foreseeable future. Unfortunately the party seemed all set to continue indefinitely, she noted glumly, an hour or so later. Then she noticed some of the older guests making a move, and, seeing her chance to escape, Chloe hurried to help see them off. Afterwards she drew her mother aside.

'Gwen, would it be terribly bad manners if I went off to bed now? I've done my duty where the dancing's concerned——'

'My dear child, of course not,' said her mother firmly. 'You look exhausted. You've been on the go since first thing this morning. I don't know what I'd have done without you.' She gave Chloe a little push. 'You insisted *I* have a rest this afternoon, remember. Leave everything to Jess and Lisa from now on. Off you go.'

Chloe gave her mother a hug, then stole up the back stairs to make use of a bathroom while there was still peace to do so. She slipped next door to her bedroom afterwards with a deep sigh of relief, weary as she hung up the expensive sliver of dark blue satin bought for the party. She removed all traces of the rather elaborate make-up she knew had been expected of her for the occasion, took down her heavy red hair and brushed it, then slid a warm, long-sleeved nightgown over her head, wrapped herself in an ancient grey wool dressing gown and tugged on thick red wool socks. She switched off the light, drew back the curtains and pulled down the window a crack, welcoming the frosty night air after the heat and cigarette smoke of the festivities below. She smiled wryly. Normally the atmosphere in the draughty old house was on the bracing side, but tonight her mother had agreed to keep the heating on later than usual for

the benefit of guests used to city houses with modern
central heating systems.

Curling up in her usual place on the wide window seat,
Chloe gazed out at the stars, depressed to find that, bone-
weary though she might be, sleep was a long way off.
Her room was over the kitchen, looking out over the
back lawn, where moving lights from cigarettes showed
people strolling in the darkness, taking a breather from
the music which still throbbed from the front of the
house at volume since the only building within earshot
of the Parsonage was the church.

Unexpectedly her thoughts turned not, as she'd expected, to the familiar pain of heartache, but to Piers
Audley, successful barrister and cause of flutters in the
Little Compton dovecote when he had inherited Clieve
House from the elderly great-aunt who'd lived out the
last years of her life in seclusion there. Chloe smiled
wryly. How pleased her mother had been to have him
turn up tonight—his first social appearance locally, and
a definite feather in Gwen Lawrence's cap, not least because her friend Louise Dawson had failed to lure the
celebrity to her fork lunch on Boxing Day.

Piers Audley, a rising star in law circles, was also well
known to the public because so many of his clients were
celebrities in one field or another. Old Mrs Enderby, who
kept cuttings of his successes, had taken satisfaction in
telling Gwen Lawrence that her great-nephew's re-
markable skill with both witnesses and juries alike had
earned him comparison with the great Marshall Hall of
the previous century. And it had to be a man like that,
of all people, Chloe thought bitterly, who'd been the
one to eavesdrop on her stupid, melodramatic tears
behind the laurels. And to crown it all he wasn't at all
what she'd expected. In any way. Piers Audley was one

of the most attractive men she'd ever met. In other circumstances she could well have been drawn to him.
Always supposing, Chloe, she told herself acidly, that a
man like Piers Audley was likely to take any notice of
a nobody from the Shires like you.

Chloe stayed where she was for a long time, watching
the stars disappear and flakes of snow begin to feather
past the window, until she heard people beginning to
drift upstairs at last to bed. Deciding it was time to shut
out the cold and get to bed herself, she reached to push
up the window then stiffened, her own name jumping
out at her from a slurred, laughing male conversation
as two men went past beneath her window. One of them
paused to strike a match, and Chloe leaned closer to the
open sash, ignoring the cold as she discovered that some
drunken idiot was actually taking a bet from his chum
on the chances of getting into Chloe Lawrence's bed to
round off the evening.

'She's a cracking-looking girl—used to be a model,
and a right little raver, I've heard. Used to shack up with
some photographer——' There was muffled, licentious
laughter which made the furious eavesdropper long to
hurl something down on their unsuspecting heads.

The amorous suitor, she realised, outraged, was Tim
Armstrong, the trainee doctor at the practice where
Marcus was a junior partner. He'd been charm personified earlier on, apart from a tendency to crush the
life out of her during one of the slower numbers. Now,
it seemed, he'd found out where she slept, and planned
to pretend he'd mistaken her door for the bathroom if
he was seen. Once he was in her room, he assured his
friend, chortling, he was home and dry. Chloe ground
her teeth in rage. The possibility of her refusal obviously
never entered her drunken swain's conceited head.

Chloe closed the window very quietly, thought for a moment, then stuffed pillows down the centre of her double bed, tucked in her beloved old teddy bear towards the top, pulled the covers round him and slid silently from the dark bedroom to race along the dimly lit upper hall to Jessica's.

'Can I bunk in with you?' she whispered as she closed the door behind her, then stood transfixed with horror as a light went on beside the bed to reveal a very different face from Jessica's.

CHAPTER TWO

'OF COURSE. Only too delighted,' Piers Audley informed her without turning a hair, 'but no doubt you were expecting your sister.'

'You bet I was! What on earth are you doing in Jess's room?' she demanded, shock depriving her of finesse.

'The weather's now shaping up to a blizzard, no taxis to be had and all other available drivers too much over the limit with champagne. Your mother flatly refused to let me hike back to Clieve House, whereupon your sister promptly overrode my protests and gave up her room to me.' He smiled politely. 'Forgive me if I don't get up. No dressing-gown.'

In any other circumstances Chloe would have turned tail and fled back where she belonged. As it was, she sagged against the closed door, letting out a deep, despairing breath. She thrust a hand through her hair in an agony of embarrassment. 'Look, Mr Audley—Piers— now I am here, would you mind terribly if I stayed for a few minutes?'

His eyes gleamed as he managed as graceful a bow as possible in the circumstances. 'Far from minding, I hope you'll stay as long as possible. It's obvious you're in need of sanctuary again, Chloe.' He thrust a pillow behind him and sat up straight, with casual disregard for an expanse of lean brown torso. 'From what, or whom, this time? Or shouldn't I ask?'

Wishing herself a hundred miles away, Chloe explained tersely, prompting a scathing curse from the man in the bed.

'Stupid oaf,' he said with angry distaste. 'Want me to sort him out?'

'Heavens, no!' She smiled a little. 'Once he finds he's making advances to a teddy bear my Lothario will slink off to the attics where he belongs. Having lost his bet,' she added with venom, and shivered, suddenly aware she was chilled right through to the bone.

'You must be freezing,' said Piers swiftly. 'Aesthetically your home is a delight, Chloe, but it's undeniably draughty. I won't embarrass you by leaping out to offer my place, but there's a blanket folded at the end of the bed. Wrap yourself up and take the armchair over there.'

She hovered uncertainly, deeply conscious of the hint of intimacy in the situation.

'Or,' said Piers blandly, 'would you rather go in search of your sister?'

'No—not really,' said Chloe, teeth chattering, not wishing to point out that if her sister wasn't in her room she was likely to be in bed with her future husband. 'Heaven knows who I'll find roaming around.' She gave a despairing little shrug. 'If you don't mind I'll take advantage of your offer for a few minutes, at least. Mrs Dawson is sharing with my mother so I don't fancy barging in there. Imagine the fuss!'

'Vividly. Are you often besieged by importunate male guests bent on seduction?' added Piers.

Chloe swathed herself in the blanket, cheeks burning as she huddled in the comfortable old chair as bidden. 'Certainly not,' she said shortly. 'Tonight is a one-off type of situation all round. We don't party much at the Parsonage. This year Marcus and Jess thought it would be a good idea if we paid off a lot of outstanding family hospitality along with theirs, and made it a double engagement party and New Year's Eve do rolled into one. They contributed to the cost of food and Marcus and David went halves with the drinks——' Chloe stopped suddenly, giving him a wry smile. 'I'm chattering. And embarrassed. All this must sound very rustic and unsophisticated. You probably use a caterer when you entertain.'

He shrugged. 'I return hospitality at restaurants, I'm afraid. If you didn't have a caterer, who achieved the excellent supper tonight?'

'My mother, with the help of one or two friends. And me. Except for Lisa the others are all doctors. They were working today.'

There was a short, charged pause, while Chloe tried desperately to think of something to say. 'This is so difficult,' she burst out at last. 'It's such a preposterous situation.'

'Two comparative strangers alone together in a bedroom in the small hours—discussing catering arrangements.' Piers smiled into her eyes. 'As a story it would never hold up in court.'

Chloe fought back another disturbing *frisson* of excitement, and fidgeted uneasily in the depths of her cocoon of wool. 'Very true. Look—I'd better go.'

'Wait a while,' he advised. 'If you catch your would-be swain in the act, things could get out of hand. Give him time to get away. In the interim perhaps you'll be kind enough to satisfy my curiosity——'

'About why I was crying!' said Chloe, resigned.

He gave her a look of such dauntingly cold reproof that she retreated deeper into her wrappings, subdued. 'No. Despite my words earlier I respect your privacy on that subject. I was referring to your sudden retirement from the modelling world.'

Chloe stared at him, astonished. 'You knew I was a model?'

'I do now. When I saw you coming down the stairs towards me this evening I had a strong feeling of *déjà vu*, as though we'd met before. Which in a way,' he added with a faint smile, 'we had, of course, in the garden. But one look at your face and that blaze of hair made me certain I knew you. Then I overheard the teasing, realised I'd seen your face in television commercials and the mystery was solved—in part.'

'There really is no mystery,' she assured him, flushing.

'But I'm interested, just the same. And as I said earlier, it's much easier to confide in strangers.' He raised an eyebrow. 'Though for obvious reasons I no longer regard us as total strangers, Chloe.'

Her eyes dropped. 'It's not a very exciting story,' she said gruffly. 'You may be bored.'

He shook his head. 'To be honest I quite expected to be bored before I arrived. Normally I dislike New Year's Eve celebrations. But so far this one has been quite the most interesting evening I've had in a long time. So indulge me with the story of your start in modelling.'

Chloe gazed intently at her scarlet wool toes, protruding so incongruously from the pale green wool of the blanket. 'It all happened because my father died suddenly. He was the vicar here, so once he was dead we weren't entitled to live in this house any more. It was a week after my A-levels. Marcus and Jess were newly qualified.'

'So what happened next?'

'A television crew had been to my school to film for a documentary series on education and I featured in the

programme. One of the technicians told me I'd be a
natural as a model, and gave me the names of some
agencies, so I sent some photographs off as soon as I
could, without waiting for my exam results.'

'Did you expect them to be bad?'

'No. Not at all.'

Piers frowned. 'But you didn't want to go on to
university.'

'Even if I had wanted to, there was a financial
problem. My mother not only had grief to contend with
over Dad, she was utterly devastated at the thought of
leaving both her home *and* Little Compton where she'd
lived all her life. She had some money of her own, so
with what Dad left and the loan of more from my grandparents she just managed to scrape enough together to
buy the Parsonage from the church commissioners.'

'But didn't the new incumbent require the house?'

'He was provided with a modern vicarage half a mile
away.'

'And your mother was left with no money to send you
to college.'

Chloe shrugged. 'She'd have moved heaven and earth
to manage it if I'd said I wanted to go, but I insisted I
was keen on getting a job.' She smiled crookedly. 'I just
didn't let on what type of job I was after until I got it.'

'Your family didn't know what you had in mind?'

'No fear. To them I was a skinny, carrot-topped
beanpole. They'd have fallen about laughing at the very
idea.'

'So what happened next?'

'The Tempest Agency liked the photographs I sent
them, gave me an interview and took me on. And once
again my grandparents came to the rescue with the lump
sum needed to start me off for my portfolio and unex-

pected necessities like the right shoes and underwear, make-up and so on.'

From the start Chloe's career as a model had taken off like a rocket. The camera's instant, inexplicable love-affair with her bone-structure, plus her wealth of fiery hair, brought her almost overnight success. In her first three months as a model she featured in a televised fashion show and worked for three of the top fashion magazines, flying to the States for one of the shoots.

'It was all to do with luck,' Chloe said, shrugging. 'By some freak of nature I just happened to have the look they wanted that year. I was still a tall, skinny redhead, with a face that was all eyes and mouth, but the camera somehow transformed all that into a saleable commodity, and I was lucky because most of the time the camera was in the hands of a master like Mick Streeter.'

The gifted photographer had been her Svengali from the first, Chloe told her intent listener. She'd already possessed the right measurements, even the looks and stamina and determination to succeed, fuelled by the need to earn money quickly. But Mick had created the personality and charisma she needed to take her into the top ten. Her 'princess-in-the-ivory-tower persona', he called it. And once he took her in hand her face was soon on the glossiest magazine covers, her hair was selling gallons of shampoo, her graceful body was becoming well known on famous catwalks, and she was flying all over the world on fashion shoots.

'I worked so hard I didn't have time for anything else.'

'So why did you give it up?' asked Piers curiously.

'Because I wasn't cut out for it, Mr Audley,' she said very deliberately. 'From the first I never meant to stay at modelling a day longer than necessary. All the time

I was working I saved every penny I could. I earned good money almost from the start, so Marcus got some advice from a friend and invested it for me. But it took longer than I expected, and would have taken even longer, only my grandparents died within months of each other, and Mother inherited some money as well as the house in Bath they left her. When she sold it for a very good price it meant I could finally give up modelling, happy in the knowledge that we could continue at the Parsonage for life.'

'What happened then?'

'I came home, just as I'd always meant to.'

Piers Audley looked at her searchingly. 'I trust your family were suitably grateful for your efforts up to that point.'

'Of course they were. But it wasn't some noble sacrifice! I was a very normal teenager, and it was exciting at first, but only for a very short period. It soon palled, and I knew very quickly it wasn't the life for me. But I stuck at it because it just so happened I had something to sell—my looks. If Marcus or Jess had possessed anything marketable they'd have done exactly the same.' Chloe shrugged. 'Actually my family were happiest the day I gave it up. Marcus detested the whole thing, and my mother never had an easy moment the entire time I was away.'

'How about your sister?'

Chloe's eyes lit with warmth. 'Jess is very practical. When she realised the only way she could help was to give me her wholehearted support that's exactly what she did. My mother was terrified at letting her ewe-lamb loose on the wicked world, while Marcus tried everything he knew to argue me out of it, and in the end lost his famous temper and washed his hands of me for a while. It was Jess who consoled my mother by finding me a bedsitter near St Mary's, Paddington, where she did her hospital training, and it was Jess who kept tabs on me all the time I lived in London and reported to my mother regularly to make sure she didn't worry.'

'And it's Jess who's going to marry the man you're in love with,' added Piers without mercy.

Chloe breathed in sharply. 'Jess knows nothing about that,' she retorted, eyes flashing. 'Nor ever will, if I can help it.'

'I saw that for myself earlier. You're a highly accomplished actress.'

Chloe controlled her resentment. 'A successful model needs to be,' she said neutrally, then gave him a polite smile. 'I do hope I haven't bored you. Normally I keep my life story strictly to myself.'

'I'm deeply conscious of the privilege.' He returned the smile with sudden warmth. '*And* for the pleasure of seeing you with your hair hanging down and your face scrubbed clean, not to mention those preposterous socks.'

At Chloe's unwilling chuckle he nodded in approval. 'That's better!'

'I'm not always such a misery,' she assured him. 'Tonight—tonight was a strain.'

He eyed her challengingly. 'How will you cope when it comes to your sister's wedding-day?'

Her chin lifted. 'As you said earlier, Mr Audley, I can be a very good actress when the occasion calls for it.'

He raised a hand to acknowledge her thrust, and Chloe got up to go, disentangling herself from the blanket.

'Now I must get back where I belong. My misguided Romeo must surely have taken himself off by this time.'

'I haven't heard him pass,' said Piers, frowning.

Chloe shrugged. 'Probably crept upstairs hoping nobody would.' She folded the blanket and laid it across the foot of the bed, then smiled a little awkwardly. 'Thank you for letting me stay.'

'The pleasure was entirely mine,' he assured her, and held out his hand. 'Thank you for telling me your story.'

Once again the faint *frisson* of excitement warned Chloe to be careful. She took the hand rather gingerly then stiffened, shooting him a suspicious look as he drew her down to sit on the edge of the bed.

'Don't worry, Chloe,' he said curtly. 'Sanctuary comes free. No fee required.'

Her eyes fell. 'Sorry.'

'Don't be. After that dolt Armstrong's behaviour you do well to be wary.'

'Do I need to be wary of you, too?' she asked bluntly, looking up.

'If you mean am I experiencing all the normal male response to being alone in a bedroom with a beautiful woman, then I admit I'm neither a eunuch, nor made of stone!' He paused, eyes gleaming. 'However, if you cast your mind back to midnight, you may remember I made no attempt to cash in on the occasion.'

'True.' Chloe tried to pull her hand away, but he held it fast.

'Which,' went on Piers relentlessly, 'doesn't mean I didn't want one of the kisses all the other men were demanding with such enthusiasm.'

She stared at him in alarm as he bent towards her.

'I rather think I've changed my mind,' he drawled, and dropped her hand to grasp her by the shoulders. 'Perhaps I will demand a fee after all.'

This time the jolt of excitement down Chloe's spine was so intense that every nerve in her body reacted as

Piers bent his head and took possession of her mouth. For a moment she surrendered to the sheer, unexpected pleasure of his kiss before anger swept through her in a hot, resentful tide and she thrust him away.

'I might have known,' she said venomously. 'You're just the same as the rest!' She would have leapt to her feet but Piers was too quick for her. He pulled her back into his arms and kissed her again, with such force that her head was reeling when he released her and she put a hand to the bed to steady herself as she saw he was staring over her shoulder, his amber eyes frosted with hostility. Chloe scrambled off the bed hastily to gaze in dismay at David Warren, who stood rooted to the spot in the doorway, a tide of brick-red colour flooding his stunned, attractive face.

'Ah, Dr Warren. Do come in. You obviously didn't know your fiancée had turned her room over to me,' said Piers coldly.

David thrust a hand through his hair, swallowing convulsively. 'Hell, no. I've been talking shop with Marcus in his room for ages. I had no—I mean I wouldn't have dreamed——'

'You'll probably find Jess up in your bed,' said Chloe without inflection.

'Yes. Right. Well—thanks.' He backed out in a hurry. 'Can't apologise enough—damn sorry to barge in...' He fled, leaving a very pregnant silence in his wake.

'This just isn't my night,' said Chloe viciously, and retied the sash of her dressing-gown with a jerk. 'My mother tries hard to be liberal, but her young are not encouraged to cohabit with their partners under her roof until respectably married. It seems it doesn't put a stop to illicit midnight scuffles, which is why David looked so appalled.'

'He looked appalled, Chloe Lawrence,' said Piers with emphasis, 'because he found you with me.'

'If anyone was appalled it was me,' she retorted. 'David was just embarrassed at being caught trying to sneak in with Jess.'

Piers eyed her searchingly. 'Are you all right?'

'I'm absolutely fine,' she said with sarcasm. 'On top of the world. And now I really am going back to my room.'

'Not without me! Turn your back. I'll get some clothes on.'

'I don't want——' she began vehemently, then whisked round in frustration as Piers slid out of bed.

'I'm coming with you,' he said forcibly.

Chloe fidgeted as Piers quickly pulled on trousers and dress shirt.

'You can turn round now,' he told her, looking as cool and detached as though neither David Warren's interruption, nor the scene he'd interrupted, had ever happened. 'Tell me which room is yours and I'll go along and reconnoitre. You stay here.'

Recognising that argument was useless, Chloe gave him directions then slumped down in the armchair as Piers went from the room. He returned almost at once, his face grim with anger.

'Your would-be ravisher is lying flat-out on the floor by your bed in a drunken stupor. He's too large to move without disturbing half the household, so I'll take your bed for the night. You can sleep here.'

She stared at him in horror. 'But I can't let you do that—Tim will have a fit when he wakes up!'

'He certainly will. And I shall be there, ready and waiting,' promised Piers, with a look in his eye which boded ill for the importunate Mr Armstrong.

'Why?' she demanded. 'What's it got to do with you?'

'It's probably something to do with my calling,' he said smoothly. 'I hate to see crime go unpunished.'

'Including your own?'

His eyes gleamed gold with mockery. 'If the kiss was a crime, Chloe, insomnia will be my punishment for it.'

They looked at each other in silence for a moment, then Chloe's eyes narrowed to a blue gleam. 'I almost pity Tim—imagine his reaction when he wakes up to find himself at the mercy of prosecuting counsel!'

Piers answering smile made her shiver. 'I specialise in defence, as it happens, but not in this case. I can safely promise you he'll never trouble you again, Chloe. Now try to get some sleep. You look exhausted.'

'It hardly seems worth it.' She glanced at her watch, depressed. 'In an hour or two it'll be time to get up and start breakfast.'

'If you'll take my advice you'll stay in bed. Let your sister help your mother in the morning,' he advised. 'Leave the explanations to me and keep well out of the way until I've settled Armstrong's hash.'

Despite the high-handed way in which he made it, Chloe found his suggestion deeply appealing. 'You know, I rather think I will. Goodnight. And thank you. I'm sorry for bursting in on you like that.'

Their eyes met.

Piers gave her a slow, disquieting smile. 'Given the choice, only a fool would prefer sleep to such ravishing disruption. Goodnight, Niobe.'

Once she was alone exhaustion hit Chloe for six. The need for sleep was so overwhelming that she crawled into Jess's bed just as she was, socks and dressing-gown as well, vaguely registering the fact that the bed was still slightly warm from its previous occupant before she surrendered to the luxury of total oblivion. Eventually she surfaced muzzily, aware of voices in the distance, but the effort to wake up completely was too much, and she let herself slide back into the warm, welcoming void.

'Wake up, sleepyhead,' said a relentless voice.

Chloe obeyed unwillingly, raising leaden eyelids to see Jessica's animated face hanging over her.

'What's up?' she muttered irritably, and yawned, rubbing her eyes.

'I've brought you some tea,' said Jess, her eyes bright with relish. 'You've missed all the fun.'

Finding herself in Jessica's bed brought instant recall. 'Fun?' said Chloe sharply, sitting bolt upright.

Jess perched on the edge of the bed, grinning. 'Come off it, Miss Innocent. I heard all about your little *tête-à-tête* with our legal eagle in here last night. Who's a naughty girl, then? David was in a right old state when he finally ran me to earth, too embarrassed for words after finding you together.'

'Piers Audley and I were not so much together as merely in the same room,' corrected Chloe, and enlightened Jess as to how she came to be there in the first place.

'Oh, I see. I see!' Jess threw back her head and roared with laughter.

'Do you *mind*?' demanded Chloe crossly, putting a hand to her head. 'I feel horribly fragile.'

'As well you might,' gasped Jess. 'Not that you can possibly feel worse than Tim Armstrong.'

'What happened?'

'To begin at the beginning, my pet, Marcus took you up a cup of tea this morning.'

Chloe eyed her sister in horror. 'You're joking! He's never done that in his life before.'

'Must be one of his New Year resolutions. Said he thought you overdid things yesterday, and Lisa could just get her finger out this morning.'

'I bet she loved that!'

'Well, he didn't use quite those words, and followed it up with a cuddle so she didn't seem too put out.'

'Never mind all that, Jess. Was—was my bedroom occupied when Marcus got there?'

'Not so much occupied as overcrowded!' Jess fought with rising mirth. 'Apparently Piers Audley was sitting fully dressed by your window, reading *Bleak House*, with Tim Armstrong still flat out on the floor, snoring his head off.'

Chloe buried her head in her hands in despair. 'What happened next?'

Piers Audley, Jess told her gleefully, bade Marcus a courteous good morning, gave a succinct explanation of his presence in Chloe's room, whereupon Marcus wrung his hand in gratitude then hauled Tim Armstrong to his feet and dragged him downstairs and out into the garden by the scruff of his neck, with Piers and David in close attendance. Jess wasn't completely sure of what happened after that, except that Piers Audley gave the miscreant a dressing-down vitriolic enough to burn Tim's ears off.

'Only David didn't say "ears",' gurgled Jess. 'After that Tim threw up—lucky for him—so Marcus wasn't able to thump him after all.'

'And a Happy New Year to all concerned,' groaned Chloe. 'Piers Audley must be rueing the day he ever set foot in this house.'

'No he's not,' said Jess briskly. 'When Marcus drove him to Clieve House he said he hadn't enjoyed himself so much in years.'

Chloe's face lit up. 'He's gone?'

'Yes, my pet. So has Tim Armstrong. Wise lad. Driving home through the snow with the worst hangover of his entire life was a far better move than lingering in Marcus's vicinity.' Jess's big dark eyes sparkled. 'I'd love to be a fly on the wall when they get back to work together.'

'And I suppose Marcus blames me.'

Jess frowned impatiently. 'It isn't your fault, goose! Tim Armstrong's to blame—or Marcus is, for inviting him. Now go back to your room, get into bed and I'll bring you some breakfast. Marcus was quite right when he said you worked too hard yesterday. The family vote was unanimous. You stay in bed until we've fed the stragglers breakfast and sent them on their way.' She got up and took Chloe's mug, grinning. 'Mrs Dawson's determined to be last to go.'

'Then I will, with grateful thanks!' Chloe slid out of bed and hugged Jess, who looked her up and down, shaking her head.

'Heavens above, Chloe! Were you dressed like that when you barged in on Piers?'

Chloe bent to pull up her thick red socks, giggling. 'Certainly was.'

'Dear, oh, dear! I'd love to have seen his face. That dressing-gown's quite horrible. Shame Tim Armstrong didn't get an eyeful of you in it. Might have saved a whole lot of trouble.'

Chloe grinned as they went back to her room, then sobered suddenly. 'By the way, does Gwen know about this?'

'Happily, no. She came down after the men had done their hatchet job on Tim.' Jess gave her a pleading look. 'And for heaven's sake don't let on where I spent last night, either—she thinks I shared with you. Thirty-something I may be, and a fully qualified doctor with it, but I see no need to upset Gwen on that subject. So just pop between your sheets and pretend I was there with you all night. OK?'

'Oh, I see! Breakfast in bed's a bribe to stop me ratting on you.'

'No, love.' Suddenly Jess was serious. 'I agree with Marcus. You looked gorgeous last night, but by the time you went to bed you also looked fit to drop. I just hope you're not coming down with something.'

Chloe smiled as she waved Jessica away, assuring her there was nothing physically wrong that a couple of hours' peace and quiet wouldn't put right. That the heart trouble she suffered from was less easy to treat was something she kept, as usual, strictly to herself.

CHAPTER THREE

BY THE time Chloe went downstairs, shortly after midday, all the overnight guests had gone. The house was quiet as a sepulchre as she went along the passage to the kitchen, where Marcus sat alone at the table.

'Where are the others?' asked Chloe uneasily.

'Getting some fresh air for lunch, at my suggestion. I stayed behind to talk to you.' Marcus's face looked dauntingly stern as he pulled out a chair for her. 'Sit down please, Chloe.'

'Gosh, that sounds ominous!' she said lightly, obeying. 'Am I about to be hauled over the coals by big brother?'

'Not exactly.' Marcus sat down again at the head of the table, his dark eyes boring into hers. 'But, as you know, I made a hell of a scene earlier on your behalf. Now I've had time to simmer down I want to know if I was justified.'

Chloe's eyes narrowed. 'Justified?'

He scowled in the way she knew so well. 'I acted on instinct when I dragged Tim out of your room, but since then I've had time to think, and wonder——' He halted, his jaw tightening at her scornful smile.

'Oh, I see!' she said scathingly. 'Now you're wondering if he had some right to be there, that I hinted I'd fancy some fun and games to round off the evening! Did he *say* that?'

Marcus reddened. 'No. After Audley finished reading the riot act Tim just managed to blurt an apology before throwing up behind a bush. I could hardly thrash someone in that state.'

Chloe glared at him. 'And now you're glad you didn't thrash him because you're wondering if it wasn't my fault after all.'

'It wouldn't be the first time I've had to frighten someone off where you're concerned.' He jumped up and went to the window, his large frame blocking out the pale, wintry light. 'From the moment you started that blasted modelling men have been a problem where you're concerned. Except for Mick Streeter. You probably don't even realise when you're giving a come-on.'

Chloe stared at his back, outraged. 'Do you really think I'm an idiot? I wasn't throwing out any lures to Tim Armstrong—or anyone else—last night. I worked like a slave all day with Gwen for *your* party, I'd remind you, not to mention doing my best to make it go afterwards, and finally I went to bed. Alone and *very* tired. Frankly, Marcus, I bitterly resent your attitude.'

He swung round, throwing out his hands. 'Sorry, Chlo, but I had to ask. I work with Tim, remember——'

The ice in her eyes stopped him mid-sentence. 'And you chaps stick together, of course. Forget the fact that he was proposing to molest me, or that I was forced into the most embarrassing situation of my life when I barged in on Piers Audley in Jess's room to escape the idiot. You and Tim are colleagues, and boys will be boys and all that!'

'Oh, come on, Chloe. As Lisa said, you might have misled him quite innocently.'

There was a taut, simmering silence. 'I see,' she said tightly at last. 'I might have known it wasn't your idea.'

'Lisa was absolutely right to mention it,' he snapped, colouring. 'I'd have looked a right fool if I'd got the wrong end of the stick.'

'Which, of course, is all you're worried about!' Chloe jumped up, eyes flashing as she brushed past him to fill the kettle. 'Amazing, really, that a perfect stranger like Piers Audley never doubted me for a moment, while you——'

'Oh, come on, Chlo, I didn't either—not really.'

'Until Lisa planted the seed! Oh, just get out of here, Marcus. Leave me in peace to make lunch,' she said angrily.

'Let me help——' Marcus backed away involuntarily at the look in her eye. 'All right, all right, keep your hair on, spitfire. I'm going.'

By the time the walkers returned Chloe had both lunch and herself well in hand. She was even able to greet Lisa with something like equanimity.

'Oh, darling,' said Gwen Lawrence, stricken. 'We didn't mean you to do all this by yourself. But Marcus sent us all off for a walk when the sun came out because he says he never gets much chance of a chat with you these days.'

'His chat didn't take long, love, so I got on with the meal.' Chloe smiled cheerfully. 'I promise it didn't take much effort to throw a few leftovers on the table.'

'Where is Marcus?' asked Lisa uneasily, edging towards the passage door.

'No idea. Go and look for him—tell him lunch is ready.'

'How did the chat go?' muttered Jess as Gwen went off to hang up her coat.

'Marcus thought Tim Armstrong might have been in my boudoir by invitation.'

David's eyebrows shot into his hair. 'Then what were you supposed to be doing with Audley?'

'Catching you red-handed for one thing!' said Jess, slicing bread. 'This is all Lisa's doing, of course. But believe me, Chlo, Marcus wasn't giving Tim the benefit of any doubt first thing this morning.'

'He looked ready to murder the poor devil,' agreed David, helping himself to a stick of celery. 'Mind you, I'd rather have had your brother's fist in my face than the ear-bashing Tim got from Piers Audley.' He shuddered graphically. 'No wonder the bloke was sick. I was almost sorry for him.'

'Were you really?' snapped Chloe.

David put his arm round her. 'I said almost, sweetheart. I know perfectly well you weren't giving the fool any encouragement, Chloe—it's like trying to cuddle a poker right now! Which doesn't deter the majority of blokes from trying it on just the same. With you it's invariably a case of more sinned against than sinning——'

'Shut up about sinning,' hissed Jess. 'Gwen's coming.'

Chloe was heartily glad the snow hadn't lain long. The two cars drove off in convoy a couple of hours after lunch, leaving the Parsonage to its habitual peace and quiet.

'You'll find it flat for a while now we're on our own again,' commented Gwen Lawrence as they turned back into the house.

'Not flat—blissful,' contradicted Chloe with a yawn. 'Let's just laze around today. I'll help you sort the house out properly long before I go back to work.'

'I'll miss you,' said her mother, as they settled themselves with a tea-tray in front of the sitting-room fire. 'I've loved having you at home over Christmas.'

Chloe nodded drowsily. 'I've enjoyed it too. But I'll be glad to get back to the grind, oddly enough. Now I've risen to the heights of PA to the marketing director life should be quite challenging. And my promotion means a raise, remember. Very handy for Jess's wedding.'

'Only for buying your own clothes!' said her mother at once. 'You save your money for your own wedding, darling.'

'Waste of time, Mrs Lawrence. Matrimony doesn't appeal to little Chloe.'

'Someone will come along one day to change your mind,' said her mother comfortably.

Chloe accepted a cup of tea without comment, deeply grateful that Gwen had no idea the someone in question had already come along, even less of his identity.

The day before Chloe was due back in work the weather was crisp and dry with a cold, bright sun. Mrs Lawrence went to early communion and afterwards Chloe helped prepare the roast lunch they always ate on Sundays. Later Gwen went off to take tea with Mrs Dawson, and Chloe, dressed for the cold in sturdy walking shoes, her old sheepskin over a yellow sweater and brown cords, pulled a chunky brown knitted beret over her bright hair, and went out for a long walk.

She left the garden by the wicket gate Piers Audley had used when he surprised her behind the laurels, crossed the bridge over the stream beyond it, and set out on a footpath which led across fields towards the River Wye. The path led up steeply in places for a mile or two before taking Chloe along the main road towards a gate

which gave access to one of the many public paths
through the Forest of Dean.

Chloe walked briskly through woodland and across
fields with hedgerows spangled with frost unaffected by
the January sun. She exchanged greetings with people
she met along the way, some of them well known to her,
others not, most of them with happy, panting dogs in
tow, out for the exercise. Eventually she reached a
vantage point which gave her a breathtaking view of
Tintern Abbey far below in the distance and sat down
for a breather on a tree root to enjoy it for a few minutes.
Afterwards she set off along a path she rarely took because it added a good two miles to the way back home.
But today, decided Chloe, she needed the exercise. And
solitude to reflect on the surprising discovery that at long,
long last she was beginning to come to terms with a future
where the man she loved belonged irrevocably to
someone else.

She quickened her pace as she saw the pale, wintry
sun nearing the horizon sooner than expected. She swung
her long legs over a stile, then stopped in her tracks as
two large black dogs burst through a gap in the black-
thorn hedge and hurled themselves at her in flagrant dis-
obedience to the voice bawling at them to bring them to
heel. Chloe bent down, laughing, letting the two rough,
ecstatic tongues lick her hands as she fondled the satiny
heads of the retrievers.

'Hello, Boney, hello, Duke! How are you, boys?
Haven't seen you for a while. Where's Ted? I hope you
two aren't playing hookey!' She looked up with a smile
as a man thrust himself through the gap in the hedge,
then stiffened as instead of Ted Scott, as she'd expected,
Piers Audley sprinted towards her, brandishing
two leashes.

'I do apologise——' he panted, then stopped short.
'Chloe!'

She rose to her feet, forcing a smile. 'Why Mr
Audley—Piers, what a surprise.'

'Indeed.' His answering smile was equally cool. 'I
didn't recognise you—couldn't see you for dogs. You
look very different from our last meeting,' he added
deliberately.

'As well I might,' she countered tartly. 'I rarely go for
walks in my dressing-gown.'

He shook his head. 'I own to indelible memories of
certain red socks, it's true, but it was the dress I had in
mind.'

'I don't go for walks in that kind of thing either,' she
assured him and waved at the dogs. 'I assumed these
chaps had got out, or Ted Scott was somewhere in the
vicinity. And I thought you went straight back to
London,' she added, deciding Piers Audley in heavy
sweater and workmanlike cords looked bigger and more
formidable than in the black tie formality of the party.

'I did. But I drove back here this morning to see Mrs
Scott, the housekeeper. I've got something of a crisis on
my hands at Clieve House.'

'She's not ill, is she?' said Chloe quickly.

Piers shook his head, gesturing at the two panting dogs
lying at Chloe's feet. 'It's these fellows. Ted's found a
job over in Bristol, which means he can't look after them.
Mrs Scott's arthritis doesn't allow for exercising dogs
and the girl who helps with the housework is too timid
to cope with them. The dogs are off their food and Mrs
Scott is worried to death about them, so she asked me
to come back again to solve the problem.'

Chloe eyed him with growing dismay. 'You're not
going to put them down!'

'I certainly hope it doesn't come to that.' Piers looked down at the dogs with a frown. 'I live in Gray's Inn Road near the Temple, but I'm out most of the day, which wouldn't do for two large, active chaps like these. They were my aunt's dogs legally, of course, but in every other way they were Ted Scott's. Now he's gone it's a problem. They didn't react to my aunt's death at all, but they're pining badly for Ted.'

'Oh, you poor lads!' Chloe crouched down again to hug the handsome dogs, looking up at Piers in fierce entreaty. 'Can't you find them a home?'

'I wish I could, but Mrs Scott can't find anyone willing to take on both of them. And it would be kinder to put them down than separate them.'

'Oh, don't do that—please!' Chloe sprang to her feet. 'Let me talk to my mother. She knows everyone in the parish. There must be someone willing to take them.'

'I'd be eternally grateful.' Piers smiled politely. 'I'd ask you back to the house for tea, but I told Mrs Scott to lie down for a rest while I'm out, and I wouldn't know where to begin to provide you with it myself.'

Chloe raised an amused eyebrow. 'You mean you can't make tea?'

'Not at all,' he retorted. 'I'd just find it difficult at Clieve House.' His face set. 'Would it surprise you to know I loathe the place?'

'Not much. I've never been there myself, but Gwen says it's a gloomy old house. Once Mrs Enderby became a total recluse I think my mother was the only person who ever set foot in there, apart from Mrs Scott and Ivy Pascoe.'

'I know. I'm very grateful to your mother.' Piers bent to clip the leashes to the dogs' collars. 'To be honest, that's why I accepted her invitation. It seemed the least I could do to return her kindness to my aunt.'

Chloe smiled challengingly. 'So you knew your acceptance would be doing her a kindness, then!'

His jaw tightened. 'Not exactly. I merely thought she might be pleased since I'd been unable to accept any other local hospitality.' He fell in beside her, dogs in tow, as they began to walk back along the path.

'Unable or unwilling?'

'I live in London,' he reminded her. 'I wasn't here over Christmas. But I came down to see my aunt's solicitors here on the thirty-first, so it seemed churlish to refuse your mother for no good reason.' He glanced down at her. 'Not, Miss Lawrence, that I ever dreamed the evening would provide such sustained dramatic interest from start to finish.'

She gave him a kindling look. 'You mean as free entertainment it was amazing value all round.'

Piers stopped suddenly, hauling on the dogs' leads. 'I wasn't referring to your tears. But I very much enjoyed the Cinderella-like apparition in my room in the small hours, not to mention the kiss I exacted as toll.'

Chloe glared at him. 'Did you have to bring that up?'

'Why not? Any man with red blood in his veins would have done the same in the circumstances. Especially since my intruder was the ravishing Chloe Lawrence, one-time darling of the modelling world.'

'So if I'd been a plain, gawky girl with a weight problem you'd have sent me packing back to Tim Armstrong to chance my luck,' she said bitterly.

'Ah, but if you'd fitted such a description,' he pointed out with irritating accuracy, 'there'd have been no problem with Armstrong in the first place.' He smiled, his eyes glittering coldly. 'Which would have deprived

me of the episode with the young fool next morning—
something I wouldn't have missed for the world. A good
thing there was so much medical expertise on hand.'

She frowned, swallowing her resentment. 'Surely Tim
wasn't that ill?'

'I was thinking more of your brother. He was in such
a tearing rage I feared for his blood-pressure.'

'Marcus is notorious for his temper.' Chloe gazed at
the dogs with troubled eyes. 'Look, do you feel ener-
getic enough to walk back to the Parsonage with me? It
would do these lads good, and Gwen should be back by
then from Mrs Dawson's. She might have some bright
ideas about Boney and Duke.'

A gleam lit the hooded amber eyes. 'An offer I can't
refuse, Chloe.'

Taking charge of a dog each, they resumed their walk,
the traumas of their previous encounter too fresh in her
mind for Chloe to feel perfectly comfortable in Piers
Audley's company. After a while, when Piers offered
her a penny for her thoughts, she surprised herself by
confessing the reason for her constraint.

He gave her a long, considering look. 'A good thing
I'm a man of the law, Chloe Lawrence, otherwise I could
go in for a nice line in blackmail where you're concerned.'

'Wouldn't do you much good. All my modelling
money is spoken for.'

'Who said anything about money?'

She eyed him narrowly, trying to read his expression
in the failing light. 'I don't think I'll ask about the
alternative. So far we're achieving some sort of surface
amity. I hesitate to spoil it.'

'If you're tarring me with the same brush as young
Armstrong, not guilty, Chloe.' He shrugged, tugging

Duke away from a bush he was investigating. 'And don't worry, I was joking about the blackmail.'

'Good—because if I get any threatening letters you'll be prime suspect. No one else in the world is privy to my guilty secret.'

He gave her another searching look. 'I could be wrong, of course, but something tells me you've adjusted sligtly on that subject.'

She nodded briskly. 'Yes. I have. I suppose right up until the official engagement I couldn't quite quench a little glimmer of hope. But now it's snuffed out for good. I've just got to learn acceptance. We take to the main road for a short distance here, by the way,' Chloe added, and handed Boney's lead to Piers so she could swing herself over, then took charge of both dogs as Piers followed suit. For the rest of the downhill walk to the Parsonage they kept to impersonal topics, Chloe taking refuge in pointing out the homes of various people Piers had met at the party before they turned into the long, slightly overgrown driveway which led down to the house.

'We're very messy about the feet and paws,' Piers pointed out. 'It wouldn't do to get muddy prints on your mother's carpet.'

'Don't worry. We'll keep to the kitchen. Though Gwen will probably scold when she gets back.' Chloe gave him a mocking smile as she unlocked the back door. 'If I give you tea she'll expect me to get out the best cups and entertain our local celebrity with due pomp and ceremony.'

She ushered him into the back entry, handing him an old towel to wipe the dogs' paws.

'Thank you.' He shrugged dismissively. 'But I'm no celebrity. It's my clients who suffer from fame. Some of it, like pitch, tends to stick now and then to defending counsel.'

'And I bet you look great in a wig and gown, too,' mocked Chloe as she opened the kitchen door with a flourish. 'Do come in.'

The Parsonage kitchen, like the rest of the house, was a little on the shabby side, but with an atmosphere of welcome Piers Audley reacted to with undisguised pleasure as the warmth from the Aga came to greet them. The room was large and square, with stone-flagged floor and a pine table surrounded by chairs with scuffed leather seats. The sink and fitted cupboards were relatively modern, but a big Welsh dresser dominated the room, displaying a few treasured plates along with everyday china, a bowl of fruit, a dried flower arrangement, rows of photographs, a big memo pad and piles of Christmas cards waiting for Gwen to cut up into next year's gift tags. The warm air held lingering memories of the lunchtime roast, mingled with the scent from bunches of rosemary and sage hung up to dry from a row of hooks along the central beam.

'This is exactly how a kitchen should be,' said Piers in approval. 'Mine in London lacks a soul.'

'Do you cook in it?' asked Chloe, filling the kettle.

'As little as possible.' Piers sat down at the table with the panting dogs at his feet, his face losing some of the guarded look it had worn since first catching sight of her.

The dogs followed her eagerly as she set two plastic bowls of water near the door.

'Can I give them a biscuit?' she asked, and Piers shrugged.

'Whatever you like. They haven't eaten much lately.'

The dogs polished off all the water biscuits Chloe offered, enthusiasm evident in the wagging of their plumy tails.

'They must have been hungry after the walk—they saw those off pretty quickly.' Chloe looked at Piers in enquiry as the dogs settled themselves again at his feet. 'Now how about you? Did you have much lunch?'

'I ate a ploughman's at a pub en route to save Mrs Scott the trouble. And I told her not to bother about dinner. I'm leaving early for London this evening.'

'Then would you say yes to a sandwich?'

For a moment she thought he'd refuse, then he nodded politely. 'I would, indeed, if it's not putting you to too much trouble.'

'If it had been I wouldn't have offered.' She smiled sweetly. 'Even brainless models like me can rise to the odd sandwich, you know.'

'I never had the least doubt about your brain,' he assured her, unmoved, and smiled slowly. 'Even though it functions behind such a stunningly attractive exterior.'

Chloe stared at him for a moment, wishing she could summon up some brilliant, withering retort, then turned away to the kitchen counter, noting from the corner of her eye that Piers stretched out his long legs, looking very much at ease as he watched her take bread from a bin and begin to slice it.

'Actually I intended to call in on you later on my way back to town.'

Chloe, startled, kept her eyes firmly on her task. 'Really? Why?'

'Just to see how you were. Is that so astonishing?'

'Well, yes, it is rather. After the other night I'd have thought you'd had a surfeit of Lawrences, me most of all.'

'Chloe, I assure you the entire situation here that night was so intriguing I deeply regretted having to leave for London next day. Besides,' he added smoothly, 'certain aspects of that night must have made it clear I was interested in *you*.'

She stiffened, keeping her eyes on her task. 'Certainly not. I was too embarrassed by the way we met to think about it—besides, I'm notoriously bad at these things. I hadn't a clue what Tim Armstrong was working up to, remember. Though I had the devil's own job next day, convincing Marcus I hadn't invited Tim to my room in the first place. As if I would!' She gave a little shudder of distaste and brandished the carving knife at a frowning Piers. 'Beef and horseradish sauce do you?'

'Perfect,' he said absently. 'But you surprise me. There was no trace of doubt in your brother's mind first thing that morning. He looked ready to murder young Armstrong.'

'That was before Lisa planted the seed of doubt in his brain,' she told him, carving thin slices of beef.

'Ah! I see.'

Chloe provided her guest with plate and napkin, set a platter of sandwiches on the table alongside one of her mother's renowned fruitcakes, and sat down to pour tea.

'Did he change his mind eventually?' asked Piers, eating with relish.

'I think so. The atmosphere wasn't exactly cordial between us when he left, but that's nothing unusual.'

'Natural sibling antagonism.'

'Something like that. Do you have any siblings?' she added, keen to change the subject.

'No. I arrived alone and late on the family scene. So late, unfortunately, that my parents never lived to see me as a fully fledged barrister. They both died during my pupillage year.'

'That's sad.' Chloe pushed the sandwich platter towards him. 'Do help yourself.'

Piers needed no persuasion. He finished off all the sandwiches and a slice of fruitcake before Chloe, on impulse, asked if he was married.

He put down his cup with some deliberation, his eyes narrowed as they met hers. 'No, Chloe, I'm not. Surely you must have found that out via the village grapevine?'

'No,' she said with dignity. 'The subject never came up.'

'If I had been, surely you'd have found my behaviour on New Year's Eve rather strange?'

She gave him a cynical smile. 'Not at all. Past experience has taught me to be even more wary of married men than the single variety.'

'I can well believe it!' He shrugged. 'I stumbled on the secret of your single status early on, but there's no real reason for mine. I had the usual quota of girlfriends in my Cambridge days, and two or three significant relationships since which could have ended in marriage. But somehow they didn't, even though one was with the daughter of a rather eminent judge.'

'Surely that would have been highly suitable?'

'Very. Nevertheless she found someone who filled her requirements more exactly than I did.'

Chloe looked at him curiously. 'What did he have going for him that you didn't?'

'The fact that he was head over heels in love with Maxine,' said Piers without emotion. 'She told me she doubted my capacity to fall madly in love with anyone. On reflection I decided she was right. Added to Maxine's considerable physical attributes, she has a good brain, and I liked and respected her. But I wasn't in love with her. So we parted. Amicably enough, which is all to the good, as I come in contact with her father fairly regularly in my line of business. But the consuming passion that's making life so difficult for you, Chloe, is something I've never even come near to experiencing. Nor do I want or expect to.'

'Very wise,' said Chloe lightly. 'More tea?'

'No, thanks.' Piers glanced at the clock. 'I must be on my way.'

Chloe looked up as a car drew up outside. 'That's probably Gwen. If she brings Mrs Dawson in you're doomed!'

'Is that the talkative lady who invited me to lunch?'

'That's the one.' Chloe wagged a finger at the dogs. 'Now quiet, you two, or Mrs D. will come charging in to investigate.'

To her daughter's relief Gwen Lawrence came in alone. 'Sorry I'm late, darling—why Mr Audley, what a surprise——' The rest of her words were lost as the familiar, affectionate dogs rushed to greet her. 'Goodness, what are you chaps doing here?' she asked as she fondled them, then smiled warmly as Piers pushed them away so he could shake hands with her.

'Good evening, Mrs Lawrence. Your daughter's been entertaining all three of us to tea. We met out walking earlier on.'

Chloe grinned. 'We were afraid Mrs Dawson was coming in with you.'

Her mother smiled back wickedly. 'She'll be mad as a wet hen that she didn't! How nice to see you, Mr Audley. Are you down for the weekend?'

'Only for the day on a flying visit, I'm afraid.'

'Piers came down to sort out a crisis at Clieve House,' said Chloe.

'Nothing wrong with Muriel Scott, I hope?' asked Gwen guiltily. 'What with Christmas and the party I haven't been in touch with her lately.'

Piers shook his head gravely, bending to pat the dogs' heads. 'Only her usual arthritis. It's these chaps she's worried about.' He explained the problem. 'Chloe thought you might know someone able to solve it.'

Gwen exchanged a long look with her daughter then held out her hands to the dogs, who went to her eagerly, tails wagging. 'I rather think I do, Mr Audley, as it happens. Chloe's been nagging me to get another dog ever since our old Bassett hound died a year or so ago. We'll take them, won't we, darling?'

Chloe, who had been fairly sure of her mother's reaction the moment she'd heard the dogs needed a home, smiled at her luminously. 'Of course we will.'

CHAPTER FOUR

THE addition of Supreme Emperor and Wellington Black Diamond to the Lawrence household gave a welcome boost to Chloe's secret recovery programme. Boney and Duke, thoroughbreds from their shining black heads to the tips of their tails, quickly took to Gwen and Chloe as very acceptable substitutes for the absent Ted Scott. Gwen saw to their exercise during the day, but from the start Chloe made a habit of taking the dogs out every evening the moment she got home, no matter how tired she was. When the weather was fine she took them along the local network of narrow lanes. When it rained a spirited dash round the large, informal garden did Chloe as much good as the dogs after the demands of her day at Propax Parmaceuticals.

To Chloe's surprise—and secret gratification—Piers Audley took to ringing up occasionally to enquire after the dogs. At first the calls were brief, with queries about Boney and Duke, and politely expressed hopes that caring for the dogs wasn't too much for the Lawrence ladies. Chloe found herself looking forward to the calls after a while. Reluctant though she was to admit it, even to herself, she was more attracted to Piers Audley than she'd ever expected to be to any man in the circumstances. Piers was the first man in years to rouse even the slightest flicker of interest in her, and while she was cautious in her reaction to it there was no denying her pleasure when she heard the drawling, supremely assured voice on the other end of the line from time to time. And after a while the conversations grew longer, with rather more interest displayed in Chloe than the retrievers.

'Do you ever come up to London?' Piers asked one evening.

'Not much. I had enough of the big city in my modelling days. I prefer the country.'

'But what the devil do you do with yourself, buried down there all the time?'

'I don't think of it as buried! I take my mother to the cinema in Coleford now and again. I babysit for a friend who lives nearby in the village, and sometimes I go out for a meal in Pennington with a group of friends.'

There was silence for a while, then Piers said lightly, 'Nothing on a one-to-one basis?'

'If you mean with a man, no.' She paused. 'You know why.'

'Chloe, you'll get over that one day.'

'Amen to that—unrequited love's such a drag.'

'More socialising might help.'

'I had enough of it to last me a lifetime once. In my heyday there was always some man the agency arranged for me to be seen with, or some party or film premiere to be seen at, quite apart from the occasional genuine date. My remote, other-worldly look was my trademark, but in actual fact it was sheer weariness half the time. Sleep wasn't a priority a zillion years ago, when I was young.'

'You can't be so very old now!'

'Twenty-six last November. How about you?'

'A dozen years more to the very month.' He paused for a moment. 'Chloe, I need to be at Clieve House next week for a few days. Have dinner with me one night.'

Chloe almost dropped the receiver in astonishment. She frowned at it, wondering about the motive for his invitation. What, exactly, did a successful, sophisticated barrister from London want with a girl like her? Was her once-familiar face the attraction? Her eyes narrowed. Or maybe he looked back on the intimacy of the bedroom scene as an encouraging start to a little fun and games to relieve the boredom when he was forced to spend time in the country. If so, she could soon put him right on that score! Nevertheless, whatever his reasons, she was tempted to forget her qualms and say yes, if only because he was a lot more interesting than any other man she knew. Bar one.

'Are you still there, Chloe?' he asked, sounding amused.

'Yes. I was just thinking it over.'

'At great length! Believe me, I'm suggesting nothing more sinister than dinner.'

'In that case, why not?' she said casually. 'Thank you. Give me a ring when you're down.'

From the start Gwen Lawrence had exercised admirable restraint about the telephone calls, and made no comment other than to say how nice of Piers Audley to be so concerned about the dogs. 'Has he said anything about Clieve House?' she asked when Chloe came into the kitchen after the call.

'Not to me.' Chloe sat down, yawning, as her mother put the meal on the table. 'Why?'

'Rumour has it that he intends putting it up for sale.'

'Good move. He can hardly want that huge old house for a weekend retreat.'

'Pity though,' said her mother pensively.

Chloe raised a quizzical eyebrow. 'Why?'

'If he sells it, there'll be no reason for him to come to Little Compton any more,' said Gwen bluntly as she handed the vegetables. 'And there's poor old Muriel Scott, too, not to mention Ivy Pascoe. I wonder what'll happen to them?'

'He's coming down next week for a few days, so if you really want me to I'll enquire. He's asked me out to dinner.'

Gwen dropped a serving spoon. 'And you said yes?'

Chloe grinned. 'To dinner, not a proposal of marriage!'

Her mother sniffed. 'I can be forgiven for my surprise. It's unnatural the way you keep turning down invitations. No one will bother eventually.'

'A thought which struck me as I was about to refuse,' agreed Chloe. 'So I didn't.'

True to his word, Piers Audley rang Chloe the day before leaving London for Little Compton. 'I achieved success sooner than expected,' he informed her, 'which means I can get down there a day earlier than expected.'

'Am I allowed to ask who you were defending?'

'You can hear all about it over dinner tomorrow night.'

'I'll look forward to it,' she said, amused by his high-handed assumption that she'd drop everything to fall in with his plans.

'Seven-thirty, then,' said Piers, and this time rang off without a word about the dogs.

Though she wouldn't have admitted it for the world, Chloe felt a glow of anticipation as she drove home through the Friday rush hour to get ready for her evening with Piers Audley, and made a silent apology for her infidelity to the man totally unaware of the need for one.

'What will you wear?' asked Gwen, when Chloe came in from her usual walk with the dogs.

'No idea,' said Chloe carelessly, hanging up the leashes. 'Piers didn't say where we were eating—probably a pub somewhere. It's rather chilly, so maybe those new trousers——'

'Not trousers, darling!'

Chloe wrinkled her nose. 'I wear skirts every day.'

'Wear that new dress,' coaxed her mother. 'It takes someone with a figure like yours to carry it off.'

'You needn't think flattery will work, you bully!' Chloe ran upstairs to run a bath, glad she'd got home in good time to get ready for the encounter. She smiled to herself as she sank into hot, perfumed water. Anyone would think she was going into battle. Her mouth tightened. It was true enough, in a way—she fought a constant battle against heartache. But it wasn't a bad idea to arm herself with the new dress, just the same. It was flattering, but not too provocative, a good choice for an evening with a man she hardly knew. With the Tim Armstrong episode still in mind it seemed prudent to avoid further wrong impressions, even with someone as mature and worldly wise as Piers Audley.

When Chloe went downstairs her mother was in the small, inviting room which had once been the Parsonage study, the dogs basking at her feet in the warmth from the fire. She looked up with a smile as her tall daughter strolled in. Chloe had piled her hair into a loose knot on the crown of her head, hung large fake crystal hearts from her ears, and with the negligent grace she'd once been so quick to learn she turned slowly full circle, then stood with hand on hip, a great swath of apricot wool trailing from her free hand.

'Well? What do you think?'

Her mother eyed the long knitted dress with approval. 'That chocolate shade looks good on you. I just wish I'd ever been able to wear those clinging knitted things.' Gwen smiled airily. 'By the way, I'll probably be in bed early tonight.'

'Why? Don't you feel well?' said Chloe, surprised.

'I'm fine. I thought you might ask Piers back for a coffee, that's all.'

'I might indeed. So why go to bed?'

'Oh, *Chloe*!' said her mother, exasperated. 'You know perfectly well why.'

'In case he might be taken with a sudden violent urge to seduce me on the sofa, I suppose! My dear transparent mother, please stop worrying over my marriage prospects. Two of your little lambs are safely on the way to the altar, so why fret over one who doesn't fancy getting in the pen yet? In fact why shouldn't I stay single all my life if I want to?' added Chloe with sudden heat.

'Darling,' said Gwen in dismay. 'Who said anything about marriage? I just want you to be happy.'

'The one certainly doesn't guarantee the other!'

'It did for me,' was the quiet reply.

Chloe dropped down on one knee beside her mother and kissed her cheek. 'I know,' she said, calming down. 'And if ever there's the slightest likelihood of achieving the same I'll be along that aisle so fast I'll mow the vicar down in the rush.'

The dogs chose to join in at that juncture, demanding their share of hugs, and the moment passed in laughter. But when the doorbell rang Gwen fixed her daughter with a bright, wicked eye. 'I shall go to bed, just the same.'

'You're incorrigible.' Chloe was still smiling when she threw open the door to Piers Audley, who took in her appearance with an unhurried, all-encompassing look, equally elegant himself in lightweight designer tweed and a rather dashing waistcoat.

'Good evening—Niobe smiling, no less!'

'New Year's resolution,' she assured him and took him along the hall to the sitting-room. 'My mother's in here with Duke and Boney.'

'Good evening, Mrs Lawrence,' said Piers warmly, shaking her hand before he petted the ecstatic retrievers. 'I hope these two aren't giving you any trouble.'

Gwen Lawrence smiled back warmly. 'None at all. I can't imagine life without them now, Mr Audley.'

'Piers, please.' He looked across at Chloe as the dogs ranged themself on either side of her near the fire. 'Highly photogenic. It's easy to see why you were top of the modelling tree.'

Chloe picked up her wrap without haste. 'An uncomfortable perch—one I was glad to vacate, believe me.' She bent to kiss her mother. 'I'll take the dogs out when I get back.'

'All right, darling.' Gwen Lawrence smiled seraphically. 'I might not be up, so I'll say goodnight now. Have a lovely evening.'

The spring night, after weeks of alternate fog and gales, was fine, with starlit skies and a mist-edged moon playing tag with the odd cloud.

'The climate's relented at last,' said Piers, as he settled Chloe in his car. 'I took a chance and booked a meal at the Walnut Tree.'

'Dear me, how impressive,' she commented, as he drove up the narrow, overhung drive to the lane. 'Though I'm surprised you fancy going so far after the trip down from London.'

'I enjoy driving. Probably because I don't do much of it in town. I make it a habit to walk to and from the Temple as much as possible. Otherwise I use taxis.' He gave her a fleeting glance as they turned out on the main Coleford Road. 'Are you a nervous passenger?'

'Me? You are speaking to someone who endured the dangers of life in the back seat when Dad was teaching Marcus and Jess to drive,' she informed him promptly.

'Simultaneously?'

'No. Marcus first, then Jess a year later.'

'There was quite a gap before you arrived. Were you by nature of an afterthought?'

'Certainly not. My advent was—according to my mother—something she'd prayed very hard for.' Chloe sent a wry smile at his profile. 'And has probably wondered why at regular intervals ever since.'

Piers drove slowly down the steep, winding descent to the Wye Bridge, giving them time to appreciate the floodlit grandeur of Chepstow castle before they halted at the traffic lights on the pretty nineteenth-century bridge which gave access to the town. As they crossed it Chloe gave him full details of how well the dogs had settled in.

'Though at first my mother was so worried they'd pine in strange surroundings she actually borrowed an intercom thing from my friend with the children. She put the speaker on her bedside table so she could hear if the dogs cried in the night.'

Piers gave a crow of laughter. 'I hope they didn't!'

'Far from pining, Boney and Duke snored their heads off so loudly Gwen couldn't get a wink of sleep! The intercom went back to Marian pretty sharpish.' Chloe settled down deeper into her seat. 'Right, now it's your turn. Tell me how many people you've sent down today.'

'I get people off, not send them down! I used to work in the criminal courts but these days my briefs are mainly libel cases. It's one of the few areas in civil law where the parties can insist on a jury.' He coughed modestly. 'I am reputed to have a certain skill with juries.'

'So I gather. I read about one of your cases in the Sunday papers not long ago,' said Chloe. 'Take the Itton turning, second one around,' she added automatically, as they approached the roundabout at Chepstow racecourse.

'Thank you.'

'You knew. Sorry.'

'Not at all. It would have been easy to miss.'

'So who did you defend this time?' asked Chloe once they were driving along the narrow road which led for several leisurely, meandering miles on its way to Raglan and the dual carriageway for Abergavenny.

'I was appearing for a commercial television channel. A lady was suing them for coupling her name with a convicted bank-robber in one of their documentaries.' Piers drove with effortless skill as he described the lady's misfortune in having a so-called friend who produced a letter from the claimant giving explicit details of a short, but colourful sexual liaison with the criminal several years before. 'Once the jury heard the details the case collapsed, of course. But Madam X refused to concede it, which meant I had no choice as to course of action.'

'You mean you cut her to ribbons!'

'I was brief and to the point, yes. Once the lady insisted on going in to bat she risked being bowled out.' He glanced at her. 'Do you keep a diary, Chloe?'

'I used to in my teens. But I'd never have the brass to bring a libel action against anyone.' She sighed. 'Not that I didn't long to sometimes in the old days. The fiction written about me in certain tabloids was unbelievable.'

'Those who knew you well ignored it, surely.'

'Well, yes. Most of them. But some of it dogs my footsteps to this day. I heard Tim Armstrong telling someone I was a "right little raver", remember. *Your* experience of eavesdropping was rather different,' she added significantly.

'Very true. If I hadn't heard your woe, Niobe, we might still be formal acquaintances.' He paused. 'On second thoughts you'd probably have come to my room just the same. And what man could resist an overture of that kind from the glamorous Miss Lawrence!'

Chloe remained civil with enormous effort. 'Glamorous was hardly the word for me on that occasion, if you cast your mind back to my school dressing-gown and thermal socks. When Jess saw me the next day she felt for you deeply.'

'Why?'

'For having had to suffer the sight of me, dressed like that. In Jessica's opinion the entire situation could have been avoided. One glimpse of me in my winter night gear would have turned Tim Armstrong off like a cold shower.'

'Which would have been a pity from my point of view,' observed Piers with emphasis. 'It's not often I get nocturnal visits from beautiful maidens seeking sanctuary. I felt rather like St George.'

'A pity I wasn't dressed for the part of damsel in distress.'

'Clothes are irrelevant to someone with looks like yours.' He glanced up at a road sign. 'Abergavenny approaches. If I remember correctly we negotiate a rather tricky roundabout at this point. Your navigating skills may be needed.'

Later, as she ate skate with black olives and fennel, followed by Toulouse chestnut pudding, the exquisite food and delightful country-inn atmosphere of the famed Walnut Tree would have been enough, alone, to make the evening agreeable to Chloe, but with Piers Audley as companion she found she was enjoying herself more than she'd done in a very long time. When she confided this, his smile was so sardonic that she frowned.

'Don't you believe me?'

'I do. But less surprise on your part would have been more gratifying, Chloe.'

'I never expect to enjoy dining with anyone,' she said flatly. 'I've tried it often enough, but I always end up pretending my companion is—someone else.'

'And tonight?'

'Tonight I haven't.'

'Not once?'

'No.'

'Look at me, Chloe.'

She raised her head to meet his searching eyes with a steady blue gaze.

'I do believe you're telling the truth,' he said at last.

'I am.'

'Then the therapy's begun to work.'

'Therapy?'

He smiled. 'I'm very grateful to your mother. When she provided a home for Boney and Duke she also gave me an excuse for ringing you up occasionally without frightening you off.'

Her eyebrows rose. 'Why should I have been frightened off?'

'Because I gather that's what usually happens when men get interested in Miss Chloe Lawrence.'

'How on earth do you know that?'

'My source is Mrs Scott.' He shrugged. 'When I gave her the glad news about Boney and Duke she was so euphoric that she talked a lot about you and your mother. She can't understand how a girl who once had her face in all the magazines, with men running after her all the time, never goes out with any of them any more.'

Chloe raised a sardonic eyebrow. 'I'd no idea my social life was so fascinating. Anyway I do go out with a man sometimes—though rarely more than once,' she added honestly.

'Your unrequiting lover has a lot to answer for.'

'Why?' she demanded fiercely. 'He doesn't know how I feel. And it's not his fault he loves someone else.'

Piers raised his hands in wry surrender. 'Pax, Chloe, pax.'

'Sorry.' She subsided, colouring. 'You mentioned therapy.'

'Right. For it to work you have to stop thinking of me as some kind of human Sword of Damocles, brandishing your guilty secret over your head. Instead look on me as a companion to spend time with occasionally, the odd walk when I'm down, or a meal like tonight. All effective therapy for the pain of——'

'Hopeless hankerings after another man,' she finished for him, and gave him a lengthy, contemplative look. 'I wonder why you're doing this?'

'I should have thought it was obvious,' he said smoothly. 'Therapy for you, pure pleasure for me.'

'Because of the way I look?' she asked swiftly.

Piers sipped his claret before answering. 'I'd be lying if I denied that your looks weren't part of the attraction.

But there's a great deal more to you than a pretty face, Chloe.'

'Thank you. Few men realise that.'

'But frankly, since there *is* a brain behind that decorative façade, it astonishes me that you don't put it to good use.'

Chloe frowned. 'I don't understand.'

Piers leaned forward. 'Wouldn't it do you the world of good as far as getting over this pointless, frustrating passion of yours if you got out into that world and did something to take your mind off it? I know you were hell-bent on getting out of the modelling world the moment you'd made enough money to retreat to the Parsonage, but surely you get tired of just vegetating there?'

Her eyes flashed. 'I do *not* vegetate——'

'What else do you call it? Burying yourself in a village in the back of beyond with only an occasional trip to the cinema sounds like sheer defeatism to me. Surely you don't want to live off your mother for the rest of your life——?'

'I do *not* live off my mother,' broke in Chloe in a furious undertone. 'Mrs Scott obviously left out a few details about me. When I gave up modelling, Mr Audley, I came home to take a course in business studies, not sit around idle all day. I've been out in the big wide world quite a while, as it happens. I even have a job. Nothing high and mighty like yours, I'll admit, but I enjoy it just the same. I happen to be personal assistant to the marketing director of Propax Pharmaceuticals in Pennington.' She rose to her feet. 'Now perhaps you'd drive me home.'

'Chloe, wait——' But Piers found himself addressing the slim, straight back of his companion as she walked with graceful haste from the dining-room and through the crowded bar of the Walnut Tree, giving him no choice other than to follow her.

But Chloe, fuming, was forced to wait in the small, flower-filled porch of the inn while Piers settled the bill, due to the fact that the stars, like the rapport between them, had vanished. It was raining so hard they had to sprint the short distance to the car. Piers threw open the door for Chloe, but her hair caught in one of his coat buttons as she tried to dive in, and by the time they were disentangled and settled in their seats both of them were wet and dishevelled and Chloe's hair was snaking down in wet coils over the sodden apricot wool of her wrap. Once the car warmed up a few miles into the journey the smell of hot damp wool was overpowering, and with an exclamation of disgust she flung the wrap on the back seat.

'Sorry about the sheep smell, I should have worn a raincoat.' Or stayed at home, she thought bitterly.

He made a dismissive gesture with one hand. 'Sorry you were drenched. But before we abandon the previous topic altogether at least let me apologise. Not that the fault is entirely mine. You've never mentioned your present job. In fact you deliberately gave me the impression you've done nothing at all with your life since you retired from modelling.'

'I certainly did not. The subject just never arose.' She breathed in deeply, still simmering with anger. 'Besides, what I do, or don't do, with my life is entirely my own business.'

'Very true. And if I've angered you I'm sorry. My sole intention was a helping hand to get you out of the rut you're in.'

'I am not in any rut,' she retorted indignantly.

'I meant emotionally, rather than career-wise.' He gave her a swift, hard glance. 'It's time you stopped day-dreaming. Forget the image your photographer friend built up. You're not a fairy-tale princess in a tower. You need shaking up—taking out of yourself, Chloe Lawrence. You're wasting your life.'

Chloe burned with resentment. 'Nevertheless it's my life,' she said tightly, after which Piers said no more and Chloe sat rigid with anger in her seat, wishing he'd chosen somewhere closer to home for their meal. The hostile silence between them deepened, almost tangible in the close confines of the car, and once they left the bypass for the slower, circuitous route from Raglan to Chepstow the journey seemed endless. As the final straw, when they reached higher ground they were enveloped in mist.

By that stage conversation would have been inadvisable even if Chloe had deigned to say anything. Piers quite plainly needed every ounce of concentration for the road ahead as visibility deteriorated to only a few yards in places. By the time they finally reached the welcome lights of Chepstow Chloe's anger had seeped away, leaving her depressed, and disappointed that the evening had gone sour on them.

'Chloe,' said Piers, as they drove through the town. 'I repeat my apology. I usually make sure of my facts.'

'Something your clients must be grateful for.'

'My motives were of the purest,' he assured her.

'You mean your sole purpose in taking me out tonight was to make me see the error of my slothful ways, I suppose,' she said acidly.

Piers chuckled. 'You know damn well it wasn't.' He looked at her as they waited for the lights at the Wye bridge. 'I asked you out tonight for the simple reason I wanted to spend time with you. Not just because you look the way you do, though lord knows that's part of it, because it's part of you. But I also like the girl behind the packaging. And I think she should come out to play more. To be specific I think she should do so with me, whenever I'm down here, as I'm obliged to be until I've disposed of Clieve House——'

'Ah, I see,' she said, enlightened. 'Now we get to the real reason. You need diversion to kill time when you're stuck down here in the back of beyond, to borrow your description.'

Piers sighed impatiently as the lights changed and he was forced to concentrate on negotiating the bridge. 'Time is too valuable to me to want to kill it, I assure you.' He slowed suddenly as the winding ascent from the bridge took them into a solid wall of fog again. 'Hell, what a night. The weather forecast was a touch secretive about this.'

'We get lots of fog, sandwiched here between the Severn and the Wye,' said Chloe, unbending. 'Though you must know that, of course.'

'Actually I don't,' he said, peering ahead. 'Before I inherited it I'd only visited Clieve House once.'

'Really? I wondered why no one seemed to know you.' Chloe looked at him curiously. 'Then you didn't know Mrs Enderby very well at all.'

'My one and only encounter with her was at the age of seven. My fond memories are of a terrifying figure in black, complete with walking stick. I smashed one of her best cups.' He smiled. 'She gave me hell, had a blazing row with my fiercely protective parents over it, and I never saw her again.'

'Then why did she leave Clieve House to you?'

'She ran out of people to cut out of her will,' said Piers caustically. 'The sole reason for my reinstatement, I gather, is my success rate in the courts of justice.'

'Careful,' she warned. 'We're almost there.'

'So we are!' Piers slowed down to turn off into Glebe Lane, and negotiated the entrance to the Parsonage drive with care. 'I almost missed it.'

'I hope you make it back safely to Clieve House. The fog's usually worse up there.' She hesitated after he'd helped her out of the car. 'If you come in for coffee it might clear later.'

Piers looked down at her quizzically. 'After all the *sturm und drang* of our recent argument are you sure you want me to?'

Chloe returned the look steadily. 'I'd hate to think of you driving off the road into a ditch on the way home.' She unlocked the door. 'If we're lucky Gwen may even have left the heating on.'

Piers shivered as he followed her in. 'For which many thanks. I still feel rather damp around the edges.' He stopped suddenly, biting back a smile as he took a look at her in the light, and Chloe sighed, resigned.

'I know I look a mess, but no time for repairs—I'd better get to Boney and Duke before they wake my mother. Will you go into the sitting-room? I'll bring you some coffee.'

'I'd rather come into the kitchen with you.'

'As you like. At least it's always warm in there.' She walked ahead of him along the passage, thrusting back her damp hair as she opened the kitchen door. 'Whoa! Steady, boys.'

Once the vociferous welcome from the retrievers had been weathered Piers sat down at the table with the dogs at his feet while Chloe filled the kettle. A coffee-tray, she noted with amusement, was sitting in readiness on one of the cupboards, complete with the best china cups and a plate of biscuits. She took a kitchen towel from a drawer and rubbed vigorously at her hair, tied it back carelessly with a piece of string then spooned instant coffee into the cups, added boiling water and took the tray to the table. She sat down opposite Piers, smiling.

'My mother's cherished Spode, no less.'

'After hearing about my experience with my great-aunt I'm surprised you're risking it.'

Chloe shook her head. 'We don't get rows for breaking things in this house. Unless we do it on purpose,' she added, and offered a biscuit.

'No, thanks. But I'd like more coffee in a minute.'

'Even this stuff? Gwen probably expected me to give you the real thing, but this is quicker. I didn't think you'd mind.'

Piers met her eyes across the table. 'Am I forgiven, Chloe? Do I take it diplomatic relations are now resumed between us?'

She looked at him consideringly. 'Is that what you want?'

'As I seem to have said before, it's by no means all I want, but I hesitate to risk your wrath again.'

'Dear me,' she said lightly, 'that sounds ominous.' She got up quickly, and held out her hand for his cup. 'If one of your wants is coffee I can supply that, if nothing else.'

Piers watched her cross the room, a gleam of appreciation in his eyes at the graceful picture she made in the narrow, clinging dress. Suddenly his eyes narrowed. 'You've lost a heart, Chloe.'

She turned to stare at him, then her hand flew to her ear. 'Oh damn—my favourite earrings. Maybe it's in your car.'

'I'll look before I go.'

Chloe handed him his coffee then sat down, eyeing him purposefully.

'What is it?' asked Piers.

'I've just remembered a question I promised Gwen I'd ask. I almost let you go without finding out. I hope you won't be offended, but she's really very anxious about your intentions.'

CHAPTER FIVE

PIERS'S eyes narrowed to a twenty-four-carat gleam. 'My intentions towards you, Chloe?'

'*What*?' She let out a gurgle of laughter. 'Good heavens, no. I meant Clieve House. Gwen's worried about Mrs Scott, and poor Ivy.'

'Ah, I see!' He smiled tantalisingly. 'My intentions, towards Clieve House and other things, will all become clear in due course, I promise you.'

Chloe eyed him, frustrated. 'But does that mean you're selling it? If so it puts the servants in a spot. Mrs Scott's really not up to keeping house for anyone else now, due to the arthritis and so on. And Ivy—well, as you must know, Ivy's a bit backward. No one else would employ her. So if you put Clieve House up for sale——'

'I'll be accused of casting Ivy and Mrs Scott out into the snow,' he said dramatically.

'Look, it may be a joke to you but it's not to us,' said Chloe heatedly. 'You're probably not used to rural communities like this, where everyone knows everyone else's affairs, but it's only natural for people like my mother to feel concerned.'

'I do appreciate that, Chloe.' Piers drank his coffee without haste, then looked at her challengingly. 'If you dine with me again tomorrow night I might just tell you what I have in mind. About Clieve House, anyway.'

Chloe frowned at him. 'And if I don't, you won't?'

'Right.'

'That's blackmail.'

'Certainly not. I see it as fair exchange.' He raised an eyebrow. 'Well? Is it a bargain? Or are you tied up tomorrow night?'

For a moment Chloe was tempted to lie and say yes, then she shrugged. 'No, I'm not.'

'Right. I'll call for you at the same time, then,' he said firmly. 'Now I'll just take these chaps for a run in the garden, then I'd better be off.'

When Chloe opened the back door she found the fog had cleared a little. She shivered and took a coat from a peg, then handed him a couple of torches. 'I'll come with you. We'll need these; the garden's an obstacle course to the unwary.'

Piers offered a steadying hand as she thrust her feet into rubber boots, then followed her out into the garden with the exuberant dogs. Once down the lawn Chloe opened the gate in the laurel hedge and led him into the paddock which formed the larger part of the Parsonage land. She let the dogs run free and stood in the open gateway with Piers, both of them keeping beams of light trained on Boney and Duke, who raced around the sodden grass, yelping and barking with delight.

'This is marvellous for them,' he said, laughing at their antics. 'Those are two happy, lucky dogs. I'm in your debt, Chloe.'

'Nonsense. We love having them. We always had a dog until old Barney died. We had a donkey, too, and a pony at one time.' Chloe sighed, drawing her sheepskin jacket closer. 'My childhood can't really have been all sun and fun, but it seems like it in retrospect. I suppose one only remembers the nice bits.'

'And you were part of a family. I envy you that. You obviously got on well together.'

'Well, mostly. Jess and I rarely had a cross word, but I used to fight cat and dog with Marcus—even worse after I got the modelling job.' She put two fingers in her mouth and let out a piercing, unladylike whistle which brought the dogs running. 'Brr—let's go in. I'll make some more coffee.'

'Is it possible that Marcus, as new head of the family, resented his little sister's sacrifice?' suggested Piers when they were back in the house.

Chloe didn't answer until they were sitting at the kitchen table, with ordinary kitchen mugs of steaming coffee in front of them.

'Perhaps,' she began slowly, 'I gave you the wrong impression. I was no martyr, Piers. In some ways I led a life that was the envy of all my friends. But they only knew about the glamorous side. Only Jess knew what a grind some of it was—learning to move and master the art of half-turns and full-turns, the dance classes, the wake-up calls at four in the morning, day-long sessions in beachwear when it was freezing, hardly ever eating a proper meal. But I was lucky, because I had Mick Streeter to watch over me. He made me take acting lessons, which gave me confidence on the catwalks and won me the television commercials. I hated the endless air travel, and the constant insecurity of it all. But I stuck at it because it was the best way to earn money to keep us all in the home we'd grown up in. All of us, the family—Marcus, Jess, Gwen and myself together. To hear Marcus at the time you'd have thought I was setting up in a less respectable line of business!' She smiled bleakly. 'Funny, really. All I wanted in life was for us to be together here. But of course we're not. Marcus and Jess both practise in the London area.'

'But the Parsonage is still their home base,' said Piers.

'Up to now,' she agreed. 'But once they marry that
will all change. Lisa has her sights set on something much
grander than Marcus's flat, and Jess and David have a
house in Ealing lined up.'

'Does this mean you feel obliged to stay at home with
your mother?'

Chloe looked up, surprised. 'Good heavens, no. My
plan didn't work out wholly as I expected, but my main
motive was always to keep my mother here where she
belonged, among her friends. That, at least, I achieved.'
She gave him a mocking smile. 'With Jess and Marcus
safely embarked on the road to matrimony my darling
mother won't be happy until she sees me dragged along
it as well. Gwen was so happy and fulfilled with marriage that she can't envisage any other goal in life for
me, too.'

'Maybe she's right.' Piers looked up from his coffee
to meet her startled look. 'By your own confession,
you're not happy with your life the way it is.' He got to
his feet briskly. 'The best way out of this emotional rut
of yours is to find some man you like, decide you have
enough in common for a firm relationship and settle for
that. It would probably last a lot longer than consum-
mation of this grand passion of yours.'

'You make it sound so easy.'

'In which case I apologise. Life is never easy, and only
the supreme optimist or the complete fool expects it to
be. Stop wasting your life—and for God's sake take that
look off your face,' he added roughly, and before she
sensed his intention pulled her out of her chair, holding
her tightly. 'No, I won't let you go,' he said, as she
struggled to get free. He raised her chin with a relentless
finger. As he saw the sudden awareness in her eyes his
own darkened. He bent his head and kissed her hard,

his arms frustrating her effort to escape. Piers kept his mouth on hers, parting her lips with a gently relentless pressure, rewarded at last as her mouth softened, and her lips parted to his coaxing tongue. Gradually resistance changed to response, and at last Chloe gave in to the now familiar spurt of excitement and melted against him, giving back kiss for kiss. Then abruptly she sagged against him as though she'd been shot. Tears welled from her closed eyes, trickling down both their faces and Piers raised his head, his hold slackening.

'Why are you crying?' he asked harshly.

Her lids flew up to reveal wet eyes blazing darkly with self-disgust. 'I didn't think I could ever *do* that.'

'Do what?'

'You know perfectly well! How can I behave like that with you when I love someone else?' She turned her head sharply, but Piers held her fast when she would have broken away.

'It's no sin, Chloe, to accept a little comfort.'

She breathed in a deep, shuddering breath. 'Kind of you to make it respectable.' She attempted a watery smile. 'Another New Year's resolution down the drain, dammit. I promised myself I'd never cry again, too.'

'If you make yourself such absurd promises, how can you possibly hope to keep them?'

Chloe sniffed hard. 'I seem to have been behaving like an idiot from the moment we met, Piers. Pity. Normally I'm quite sensible, I promise.'

'I believe you. Love makes idiots of everyone—so they say. Never having suffered the malady, I'm in no position to judge.' He smiled lazily. 'The trick is to find a cure. Marriage is the surest, according to some.'

'How you do harp on about marriage. In my book it's a dive from the frying pan into the fire.' Chloe detached herself firmly and crossed the kitchen to tear a sheet of kitchen paper from a roll. She mopped her eyes, grimaced at the mascara stains and turned to him with a wry smile. 'I must be a total wreck by this time.'

'No.' He looked at her dispassionately. 'There's some alchemy about you which overcomes drawbacks like tearstains and wet hair.'

She stared at him, arrested, then gave him a smile which made him blink. 'How very sweet of you to say so.'

'*Sweet*? No one's ever called me that before.' His smile was wry. 'I must go. Sevenish all right tomorrow?'

Chloe nodded, then hesitated, frowning. 'But I can't let you buy dinner again. Instead of going out would you like to come here for a meal?'

The heavy lids dropped to mask a gleam of surprise. 'I'd be delighted.'

'Make it eight rather than seven, then.' She waved the dogs back firmly. 'No, boys, you stay there. I can't have you bolting out through the front door at this time of night.'

Piers patted the black, shining heads, then shut them in the kitchen and followed Chloe through the hall. When she would have opened the outer door he took her in his arms again, as though the previous embrace had established a new code of behaviour. And the first touch of his mouth on hers banished all desire to resist. The desire which rose inside her instead, sharp and hot and astonishing, was a very different kind, one she responded to so fervently that she felt the clench of tension in his muscles as he held her closer. His fingers sought the nape of her neck, dispensing with the string, then they slid through her hair as he raised his head to stare down into her eyes.

'You see, Chloe?' he said softly. 'The very best therapy of all for heart trouble is this—pure, uncomplicated physical pleasure between two adults, with none of the pain and misery of your secret passion.'

She gazed up into his clever, confident face, something in his tone telling her Piers Audley was not quite as detached and self-contained as he sounded. 'You're probably right,' she agreed breathlessly, and stepped back, thrusting her hair behind her ears. 'Except for the pure bit,' she added, her eyes alight with sudden laughter.

Piers stood very still for a moment. 'The fool must be blind,' he said harshly.

Chloe went suddenly pale. 'Not blind. He—he just doesn't think of me that way.' She turned away sharply to open the door. 'Goodnight, Piers. Thank you for a truly miraculous dinner and a very—a very interesting evening all round.'

'The pleasure was all mine.' He took her chin gently and brought her face back to his. 'Though I'd like to think you derived just a little from the evening yourself.'

'Oh, I did. Otherwise not even the promise of revelations about Clieve House would tempt me to repeat it,' she assured him.

'Good. Until tomorrow evening, then, Chloe.' He touched a hand to her cheek, and strode off to the car.

She closed the door quickly, not waiting to see him off, and went back to the kitchen feeling oddly elated, her lips twitching as she wondered how her mother would react to the prospect of an unexpected dinner guest.

'You're seeing Piers again tonight?' asked Gwen Lawrence blankly over breakfast.

'Not only seeing him, but giving him dinner. Here. Do you mind?'

Gwen blinked. 'No—no, darling, of course not. Only you'll have to cook it yourself. It's my bridge night.'

Chloe gasped with horror. 'They're not coming here?'

Gwen chortled. 'You should see your face! Lucky for you it's not my turn tonight. You can have the run of the house.'

'Just the kitchen and the sitting-room will do.'

'Surely you're going to use the dining-room!'

'No fear. If I'm cooking it had better be the kitchen.'

'But darling——'

'But nothing,' said Chloe firmly. 'If I'm in charge I need my finger on the culinary pulse.'

'I could make something before I go,' offered her mother.

'Certainly not. Saturday's your day off. Just come shopping with me this morning and help me buy food I can't ruin.'

When Gwen Lawrence was ready to leave for her bridge supper that evening Chloe was reading in the morning-room in front of the fire, a glass of tonic water in her hand and the dogs at her feet, and in her mother's opinion looking remarkably relaxed in the circumstances.

It was all a pose. The trick, as Chloe actually knew quite well, was to begin preparations early and choose a menu well within her limited culinary scope. Consequently a pot of creamy carrot soup was ready, blending its various flavours of garlic and cayenne and paprika, a crisp green salad awaited its last-minute dressing, a dish of creamy dauphinoise potato slices bubbled in the oven, and some lamb cutlets crowned with sprigs of rosemary would require, according to Gwen's instructions, very few minutes under a hot grill to bring them to perfection. Nevertheless Chloe couldn't quite control a tremor of apprehension.

'I'm off now,' said Gwen, surveying the apparently relaxed, graceful figure sprawled on the sofa. 'You were determined to wear trousers tonight, then.'

Chloe looked up with a grin. 'Ah, but these are special—my combined luxury Christmas present from Jess and Marcus, remember.'

Gwen eyed the supple bronze suede doubtfully. 'I'm not saying you don't look good in them, darling, it's just that a dress would be so much more—well, suitable. Though the jersey's perfect with them. Is that the one David gave you?'

'Yes.'

'Only a man would choose pink for a redhead!' Gwen bent to kiss her daughter's cheek. 'Good luck with the meal.'

Chloe pulled a face. 'I hope I won't need it!'

'Of course you won't. By the way, you can let the potatoes carry on for at least half an hour. I just checked.'

'O, ye of little faith. Go on, shoo!'

Once she was alone Chloe's air of confidence evaporated a little. She went out to the kitchen, fiddled with the table settings, rearranged the pot of daffodils in the centre, had a look at the potatoes, tasted the soup. She took a look at herself in the hall mirror, smoothed back a lock of bright, shining hair, then met her dark blue eyes very directly. You're excited, she told herself, shaking her head. For the first time ever you're actually looking forward to spending time with a man. Piers Audley's therapy was working far more successfully than she had any intention of letting him know. When Boney and Duke barked in response to the doorbell she stood very still for a moment, suddenly visited by the memory of a hard, possessive mouth on hers in this very spot the night before. She breathed in deeply, squared her shoulders and walked briskly through the hall to let him in.

'I come bearing gifts,' Piers said, smiling, his hair gleaming under the porch light as he bent to pat the frisking, joyful retrievers.

'Does that mean I shouldn't trust you?' she parried.

'Unlike the Greeks, my gifts are mere appreciation of hospitality,' he assured her, producing a large box of chocolates. 'These are for your mother, the claret's for you. It's a good year.'

'I'll give you a corkscrew so you can let it breathe. Gwen will love the chocolates, but at the moment she's not here,' Chloe told him casually, and went ahead of him into the morning-room to put the chocolates on a shelf near her mother's chair. 'Due to our recent revels I can offer most usual things, plus some bourbon Marcus left behind at Christmas.'

'A fairly abstemious gin and tonic, please.' Piers stood in front of the fire, flanked by the dogs and shivering a little despite the fact that this time he wore the tweed jacket of the night before with a roll-neck sweater the colour of French mustard, and brown needlecord trousers vintage enough to hug his long legs closely. He took a corkscrew from her and uncorked the bottle with negligent skill. 'I walked down tonight for the exercise, but I should have worn something warmer. I always forget that it's colder down here after London.'

'It's the wide open spaces without and the high ceilings and draughts within,' said Chloe, smiling. She took the bottle from him, handed him his drink and resumed her seat on the sofa. 'When you can bear to leave the fire, do sit down. My mother asked me to pass on her apologies. It's her bridge night, so I'm afraid you're subjected to *my* cooking.'

Piers came to sit beside her. 'No disrespect to your mother, but I'd be lying if I said I was sorry to dine alone with you.'

'You may change your mind after sampling my cuisine!'

'The food is immaterial, Chloe.' He smiled slowly. 'Better a dinner of herbs and so on.'

She returned the smile, unruffled, and glanced at her watch. 'Would you like to sit here and get warm, or will you brave the rigours of the hall and come to the kitchen? I'm not brave enough to leave dinner to its own devices much longer. We're eating there, anyway, much to Gwen's disapproval.'

Piers laughed and jumped to his feet. 'Sounds good to me. The only other kitchen I'm acquainted with is my own—and I wouldn't describe the relationship as close!'

Chloe laughed as she closed the door of the sitting-room behind them. 'Ours with the Parsonage kitchen is positively intimate. We use the dining-room on state occasions only, preferably in summer. It's the coldest room in the house.'

Piers followed her to the kitchen, dogs in convoy. 'Only in temperature, Chloe. Your entire home is a warm, welcoming place, a far cry from Clieve House.' He sniffed the air appreciatively. 'Something smells good.'

'Don't expect too much,' Chloe warned, putting the claret on the table. 'If you'll sit there I'll just do the final bits.'

As she tied on a striped butcher's apron, Chloe was suddenly visited by thoughts of the previous night's exchanges as Piers sat watching her. He's the same man and I'm the same old me, she thought crossly. Why should a few kisses, a couple of fleeting moments of physical contact change things? Nevertheless she was deeply aware of intent gold eyes following her every move as she slid cutlets under the grill and put a baton of French bread in the oven to heat through.

'I won't offer to help,' said Piers, finishing his drink. 'My culinary skill extends solely to toast and the odd omelette—both of which I do supremely well, of course.'

'Egotist!' Chloe laughed and turned the heat up under the soup. 'I quite like cooking,' she admitted. 'But Gwen's such an expert I usually just peel vegetables, do the washing-up and so on.'

He laughed. 'Which sounds odd coming from a woman who once lived a life of such publicised glamour!'

Chloe turned from whisking a dressing. 'To me it was just a job that earned me money. Frankly, I'm amazed you remember me. Models come and go at a fair rate.'

'The truly memorable faces linger in the mind. Who could forget Jean Shrimpton, or Twiggy? And they were a long, long time before you,' he pointed out. 'Besides, you did some television commercials.'

'True. Hair for shampoo and my legs for stockings.' Chloe turned back hurriedly to the cutlets. 'Right. I'll just put these to keep warm and we're about there.' She transferred the cutlets to a serving dish and put them in the warming oven, then decanted soup into two bowls and carried them to the table before taking the bread from the oven. She cut it into thick slices, set the basket in the middle of the table and removed her apron. 'I'll let you pour the wine, Piers.' She shook out her napkin and sat down with a little sigh.

'I hope that's not exhaustion,' he commented, as he filled her glass.

'No. Relief.' Chloe raised her glass in toast. 'The tricky bit for the L-plate cook is getting everything ready at the same time. What shall we toast?'

Piers touched her glass with his. 'The future. And whatever it may hold.'

She smiled wryly. 'Sounds portentous. But I'll drink to that.'

Piers tasted his soup appreciatively. 'If you made this, congratulations, Chloe. *And* it matches your sweater. I wouldn't have thought pink was perfect with that hair of yours, but it is. Your taste is unerring.'

'Actually it was a gift.'

'From your sister?'

'No—from David.'

There was silence for a moment then Piers shrugged. 'His name is bound to come up occasionally, Chloe. I flatly refuse to let it put a damper on the occasion.'

She nodded. 'You're absolutely right.' She took their bowls away and quickly brought the rest of their dinner to the table.

Piers surveyed the cutlets and salad and sizzling dish of creamy, crisp-topped potatoes with respect. 'For someone who disclaims any culinary skill, Chloe, this is very impressive.'

'I'm showing off,' she admitted honestly. 'It's the best I can do, apart from the odd pasta dish.'

The evening passed very agreeably, both of them content to linger at the kitchen table long after the meal was over.

'We should go back to the sitting-room,' said Chloe lazily. 'Gwen would definitely expect me to serve coffee in there after slumming in the kitchen for dinner.'

'I notice you call your mother Gwen,' commented Piers.

Chloe nodded. 'Until I went to school I didn't know other people said "Mummy" and so on.'

'Will you want your children to do the same?' he asked.

Her face shadowed. 'Since it's unlikely I'll ever have any, the question doesn't arise.'

Piers eyed her challengingly. 'Would you like children, Chloe?'

She took her time about answering. 'I would have done,' she said carefully, 'if things had been different.'

'If you could have married the object of your hopeless passion, I take it.'

Chloe jumped to her feet, suddenly restless. 'We really must make a move to the sitting-room.'

'I'll take the dogs for a run first,' said Piers, getting up.

'In that case I'll have coffee ready when you get back.'

'Done.' Piers smiled as he clipped leashes to the enthusiastic dogs. 'Then your mother will never know that we didn't abandon the kitchen table the moment dinner was over.'

When Piers got back in, shivering with cold, Chloe had made up the sitting-room fire, and had a tray of coffee beside her, complete with a decanter of port.

'Freshly ground beans tonight,' she assured him, as he held out his long hands to the warmth. 'What have you done with the dogs?'

'I ordered them to bed.' He took a cup of coffee, poured himself a glass of port and sat down beside her, giving her rather an unnerving smile. 'What time will Mrs Lawrence be home?'

Chloe looked at her watch. 'Any time now,' she fibbed, quelling a hint of panic at the look in his eye.

Piers's mouth twitched slightly. He drank down his coffee, sipped some of the wine, then turned to Chloe, shaking his head. 'Relax. I'm past the stage where I ravish my hostess the moment dinner's over.'

Chloe glared at him. 'The thought never entered my head!'

'Tut, tut, such lies, Chloe,' he said reprovingly.

She smiled a little, some of the tension leaving her. 'But after last night——' She stopped, flushing.

Piers's eyes narrowed. 'Ah, yes. The urge to comfort which took an unexpectedly impassioned turn. And now you're worried that your invitation tonight may have given me entirely the wrong impression. Don't be, Chloe. I flatter myself I read you better than that.'

Chloe breathed out in relief, pleased to find her hand steady as she refilled their cups. 'I'm naturally wary, I'm afraid. When my face became known there were lots of men eager to be seen with me, and most of them took it for granted I was ready to leap into bed with all comers.'

Piers looked at her searchingly. 'But had your sister already met Dr Warren at this stage?'

'Oh, yes. They were students together. I was quite young when she first brought David home.'

'So every man you met afterwards was on a losing wicket anyway.'

'Not everyone. There were one or two I liked a lot—and went out with quite a bit—on my own terms.' She smiled mischievously. 'In fact my relationship with Mick Streeter was publicised quite widely at one time.'

Piers nodded. 'Even in the depths of the Temple I've heard of the successful Mick Streeter.'

'He's a good man.'

'Did you live with him?'

'No.'

'Did he want you to?'

'Yes.'

Piers shook his head. 'Don't fly into a rage, Chloe, but frankly I just can't see what it is about Warren that spoils you for the rest of the male sex.'

'Well, you wouldn't, would you?' she countered, and refilled his port glass. 'I probably wouldn't know what you saw in the judge's daughter if I met her, either.'

'True.' He raised his glass. 'To your beautiful navy blue eyes, Chloe.'

She grinned and fluttered her lashes, then sobered abruptly at the molten gleam of response in his eyes.

'Don't worry, Chloe,' he said softly, 'I'll keep my promise.'

Chloe flushed to the roots of her hair as she realised she didn't want him to, and Piers's eyes narrowed.

'Unless,' he said very distinctly, 'you release me from it.'

CHAPTER SIX

CHLOE glanced down involuntarily, sure her heartbeat must be visible through her sweater, then looked up to find Piers's eyes lingering on the curves outlined by the thin pink wool. Heat rose in her face as the heavy-lidded eyes returned to hers. Her tongue passed over her lips and she made a helpless little gesture of defeat.

'You reduce me to schoolgirl panic with practised ease, Piers,' she said resentfully, and he smiled.

'Despite your much publicised experience of men?'

'Probably because of it,' she returned acidly. 'Mick was the only one I ever felt comfortable with.'

'Because you never felt any response to his overtures?'

'To trot out the old cliché, we were just good friends.' Chloe looked him in the eye. 'As I've said before, for one very obvious reason I've never felt the least flicker of response to any man's overtures.'

Piers's eyes narrowed. 'Then have I been imagining yours to me?'

'No.' She frowned heavily. 'It's never happened before. I can't understand it.'

'You don't do much for my ego, Chloe!' He paused, eyeing her assessingly. 'Perhaps the very fact that I'm the only one in on your secret makes it easier for you to relax with me.'

'Relaxing's one thing. Behaving like—like that is something else.'

'Is your outlook due to being brought up in a parsonage, Chloe?' he said in disbelief. 'A few kisses don't count as sin!'

'I'm not a complete idiot,' she said scathingly. 'And I know perfectly well that if anyone else heard this conversation they'd think I was mad, or at the very least a museum piece.'

Piers leaned forward and took her hand. 'What's needling you, Chloe, is the fact that it's perfectly possible to enjoy my lovemaking even though you're emotionally committed to someone else. Isn't that right?'

'Not quite.' Chloe looked down at the slim, strong fingers clasping hers. 'I suppose what I'm saying is why you, rather than any one of the other men who've tried to make love to me over the years?'

'I haven't tried to make love to you yet,' he pointed out, amused.

'You know what I mean,' she said, exasperated.

One long finger smoothed the back of her hand delicately. 'Chloe, don't black my eye, but have you ever actually been kissed by the man you languish after?'

'Ugh!' She glared at him again. 'You make me sound like something out of a Tennyson poem. I do *not* languish, and of course he's never kissed me, except for a chaste peck on the cheek. What else would you like to know?'

Piers stared at her, frowning. 'How it's possible for you to be so desperately in love with someone who's never really touched you.'

Chloe's mouth tightened. 'It's obviously hard for a man like you to understand.'

'A man like me?' he pounced.

'To you attraction is solely to do with the senses. You admit yourself that your heart's never been involved, so how could you possibly understand feelings like mine?'

'You never yearn to go to bed with him?'

A tide of colour rose in Chloe's cheeks, then washed away again, leaving her eyes burning like blue flames. 'If this evening is also intended as therapy, Piers Audley, it's a total washout!'

'Then I must resort to stronger measures,' he drawled, and pulled her across his knees so abruptly that his mouth was on hers and his arms locked about her before she could utter the protest he stifled with a kiss which put a devastatingly efficient end to the argument.

For a protracted, erotic interval Chloe forgot everything other than the fiery sensations Piers Audley's hands and mouth were arousing in every part of her. Holding her open, gasping mouth captive with his relentless lips and subtle, probing tongue, he slid his hands over the thin wool outlining her breasts, his caressing fingertips lingering at the tips to tease before moving downwards over the supple suede covering her hips and thighs to travel inwards and upwards until she was shaking like a leaf even though not one inch of her was naked to his touch except her vulnerable, responsive mouth.

When Piers raised his head at last he slid a finger under her chin and raised the face she'd buried against his shoulder like a child trying to hide.

'Chloe,' he commanded. 'Look at me.'

Unwillingly her lids rose until their eyes met.

'You see?' said Piers, in a voice she'd never heard before. The drawl was gone, replaced by a hoarse intimacy which tightened muscles inside her never noticed until now. 'It is perfectly possible for a man and woman to enjoy a sexual relationship without the pain and inconvenience of being madly in love. Add to it a certain compatibility of intellect and interests and you have something worth far more than any ephemeral, passionate fling.'

Chloe swallowed and tore her eyes away. 'Utter sophistry, Piers Audley.'

'Not at all. Nothing fallacious about my reasoning, Chloe.' He caressed her hot cheek with a tracing fingertip. 'It's common sense.' He kissed her again, then set her firmly in her former place in the corner of the sofa.

'Is that the end of the lesson?' demanded Chloe breathlessly.

'For now, yes.' His smile taunted her. 'If I wasn't expecting your mother to arrive at any moment I admit I'd be tempted to carry my instruction a little farther——'

'Always supposing I was willing to co-operate,' snapped Chloe, nettled.

'You seemed perfectly willing a moment ago,' pointed out Piers with complete truth. 'Are you trying to tell me the experience wasn't pleasurable?'

She shook her head unwillingly. 'No. I'm not. It wouldn't be much use, would it?'

'None at all.' He smiled triumphantly. 'The moment I laid eyes on you I knew we'd be compatible. You dazzled me at first sight in all your party gloss, but when you burst into my room later in that terrible dressing-gown and the famous socks, it was all I could do not to pull you into bed there and then.'

'You seem very sure that I'd have accepted,' she said tartly, in command of herself again by this time. 'But all things considered it's a good thing you didn't give way to impulse.'

'If you mean Dr Warren's untimely interruption, I don't know that I agree.' His eyes took on a steely look. 'It might have served to cure him of any hankerings after his fiancée's sister once and for all, if nothing else.'

'He doesn't *have* any!' said Chloe, exasperated. 'How many times do I have to tell you that David hasn't a clue about my feelings?'

Piers's jaw set implacably. 'Forget him. Let's keep to the matter in hand.'

'Which is?'

'The relationship between you and me, Chloe Lawrence.' His eyes locked with hers. 'I'll be frank. I want you. Not only because you're a joy to look at and make love to, but because we're good together. I enjoy your company, and flatter myself you feel the same about mine, otherwise I wouldn't be here tonight. On New Year's Eve fate led me to discover why there's such a gap in your life. I give you fair warning that I intend to fill it.'

Chloe looked at him steadily, brushing back a lock of hair he'd dislodged from the tortoiseshell butterfly at the nape of her neck. 'I'm not sure,' she began with care, 'what it is you have in mind.'

'Don't be naïve, Chloe!' he mocked. 'You know perfectly well what I have in mind.'

Chloe's eyes dropped to hide her sudden rush of excitement at the prospect. 'We hardly know each other,' she said obliquely.

'A condition I intend to remedy,' he assured her swiftly. 'There's nothing to stop you coming up to London for a weekend occasionally. If you're nervous of staying at my flat I can book you a room in a hotel——' He paused, eyes narrowing. 'Now why, I wonder, does that idea find such obvious favour, Chloe?'

'Until you said that, I thought you wanted me kept in a separate compartment, labelled "for use on country weekends only",' she said tartly. 'And a hotel isn't necessary. On the rare occasions I come to London I stay in Jessica's flat.'

His eyes hardened. 'How convenient.'

Chloe raised her chin. 'David doesn't share it. At the moment Jess lives with a friend. You might have met Monica at the party—they trained together.'

'And Dr Warren has his own establishment?'

'For the time being, until the house in Ealing is ready.'

'How untypical of present-day arrangements!'

Chloe shrugged. 'The house needs a lot of basic refurbishing, like repairs to the roof and so on. Jess and David, like all doctors, are both on call regularly, which means broken nights, and days when they need to catch up on their sleep, so they decided to defer moving in until the work is finished. By which time,' she added tonelessly, 'they'll be married.'

Piers held out imperative arms, and Chloe moved towards him involuntarily, as frustrated as he when the telephone interrupted them. With a rueful smile she excused herself and hurried into the hall to learn that her mother would be home an hour later than usual. Chloe put the phone down absently, an odd little smile playing at the corners of her mouth.

'Anything wrong?' Piers asked as she rejoined him.

'No. It was my mother. Her bridge four is locked in mortal combat, apparently,' said Chloe lightly. 'They're playing an extra rubber as a decider, which means she'll be home later than expected.'

They looked at each other in silence.

'Then so will I,' said Piers softly, and Chloe smiled.

'You don't ask if I'd like you to stay.'

His mouth twisted so wryly that Chloe burst out laughing.

'It obviously never occurred to you!'

'I confess it didn't.' He glanced at his watch. 'It's early yet. Let's take the dogs out again.'

When they went into the garden the sky overhead was bright with stars but a layer of mist lay over the fields and blanked out the lights on the other side of the river. There was an eerie, hushed feel to the cold night, and Chloe gave a sudden violent shiver as she stood at the paddock gate with Piers, watching the dogs race over the frosted grass. He moved close.

'What's the matter?'

'Footsteps on my grave, I suppose.'

He put his arms round her and pulled her hard against him. 'It's time you concentrated on life, Chloe. Stop wasting it on something you can never have and settle for what you can.'

'All right, I will,' she said recklessly, and pulled his face down to hers until their mouths met. He slid his arms under her jacket until his hands locked, their faces cold in the icy air, but their seeking, communing mouths hot as he strained her so fiercely against him she thought her ribs would crack.

'Let's go back to the house,' Chloe gasped when she could, and Piers whistled to the dogs and took her hand, racing with her up the slope of the lawn with Boney and Duke in glad pursuit. They settled the retrievers down for the night in the warm kitchen, then turned out the lights and made for the blazing fire in the sitting-room in an oddly conspiratorial silence. Piers closed the door behind him then held out his arms, the molten gleam in his eyes halting Chloe in her tracks. Then he smiled, and she moved into his arms like a sleepwalker, holding up her face to his kiss as his arms closed about her.

There was something new in the embrace, she realised, an aura of possessive confidence she noted with faint misgiving.

'Piers,' she said against his mouth, and he moved back a hairsbreadth.

'Yes?'

'This—this arrangement you discussed. Do you expect me to sleep with you?'

He held her away from him to look at her.

'Of course I do,' he said bluntly. 'You're a beautiful, infinitely desirable woman, and I'm a man with all the usual hormones, so of course I want to make love to you, in every way possible. But,' he added very emphatically, 'only when you want that as much as I do. Does that answer your question?'

She nodded, reassured.

He gave a wry shrug. 'I'm discovering patience I never knew I had where you're concerned, darling. But then, I've never laid siege before to a woman who lusted after another man.'

Chloe's eyes flashed. 'Lust doesn't come into it. It's not that kind of thing.'

'Then what the hell kind of thing is it?'

She stared at him hopelessly. 'He's just all I ever wanted.'

'Well, you bloody well can't have him,' said Piers Audley with sudden savagery and hauled her back into his arms, kissing her with a force and passion which took her breath away and filled her with elation and a mounting desire she couldn't deny. Her body vibrated with response she couldn't hide from questing hands which this time slid under the thin wool tunic and the lace beneath it to find her breasts. She gasped, heat flooding her face as she felt her nipples rise to the touch of his teasing, practised fingers. She shivered, and he slid his arms around her, bending her back as his lips travelled in a lingering voyage of discovery over the taut curves of her breasts, his mouth subtle and caressing at first until suddenly she felt his lips and teeth on her nipples in a delicate torture she could hardly endure, sure he was drawing the heart out of her. Then abruptly she was free, as he put her from him and jumped up to stare down into the fire, his hands behind his back.

Chloe put herself together with clumsy, uncoordinated hands and fled from the room and up the stairs to tidy herself before her mother came home. She stared at herself in her dressing-table mirror, astonished to see a face she hardly recognised. Colour flamed along her cheekbones under eyes darkened almost to black with the force of the emotion she'd just experienced. She swallowed convulsively, brushed her tumbling hair and secured it again at the nape of her neck. She made two attempts to renew her lipstick before she was successful, then took in a deep breath and went downstairs.

Piers turned as she came in, his face inscrutable. 'I was rough. But you made me angry,' he said harshly.

She nodded, taking this for all the apology she was likely to get. 'I know.' She shrugged. 'You did ask.'

'True.'

'Are you still angry?'

'If I am, you could cure me of it very easily!'

Chloe closed her eyes for an instant against the gold flame in his. 'I would, I would, only my mother's due any moment.'

'I know.' He held out his arms. 'Come here.'

Chloe went.

They stood together in front of the fire, holding each other close, the smooth fair head bent close to the fiery hair which had once helped Chloe earn her living. Suddenly Chloe drew back to gaze up into the clever, intent face above hers.

'You haven't fulfilled your side of the bargain,' she said accusingly. 'You promised to tell me about Clieve House.'

Piers smiled indulgently. 'I was keeping that for my exit line.'

'Tell me right now—*are* you selling it?'

'No. I'm converting it.'

Chloe frowned. 'Into a hotel?'

He shook his head. 'No. Into a residential home for the elderly—where Mrs Scott and Ivy Pascoe may live free of charge for the rest of their natural lives if they so wish. Which they do,' he added smugly.

'Oh, Piers, that's such a brilliant idea!' cried Chloe, and drew his head down to hers to kiss her with such fervour that neither of them heard the car draw up until the slam of the front door had them jumping apart like a pair of guilty teenagers.

Mrs Lawrence came in looking very pleased with herself. 'Good evening, Mr Audley—Piers. I trust my daughter looked after you well.' She kissed Chloe triumphantly. 'I won a fiver, darling.'

'Who's a clever girl, then!'

'Congratulations, Mrs Lawrence.' Piers smiled warmly, exchanging a glinting look with Chloe. 'And I assure you I've been looked after quite royally. The dinner was excellent.'

Mrs Lawrence beamed, delighted, and when Piers handed her the chocolates it was plain that her cup was running over. He refused offers of more coffee or another drink, though when she heard he was about to walk back to Clieve House it took a lot of persuading to convince Gwen that he was in no need of transport home.

'No snow tonight, so the exercise will do me good,' said Piers firmly, and held out his hand. 'Goodnight, Mrs Lawrence.'

'Goodnight, Piers. I'll let Chloe see you out while I go and say goodnight to the dogs.' Gwen smiled happily, and went off to the kitchen, humming, leaving the other two in the hall, gazing at each other.

'Don't come outside,' said Piers abruptly. 'It's cold.'

'All right.' Chloe went to the door and opened it, feeling suddenly shy. 'At least it's fine,' she said, casting about for something to say.

'What would we do without the weather?' said Piers in amusement, and turned her face up to his under the lamp hanging from the Gothic arch of the porch. 'Thank you for dinner.'

'Thank you for the wine,' she returned.

Their eyes held.

Piers let out a deep breath and bent his head at the exact moment Chloe raised her mouth for his kiss, which lengthened and grew more impassioned as she locked her hands behind his neck and responded with a heat she'd never experienced in her life before.

'If we avoid a certain subject in future,' Piers drawled unsteadily when he released her, 'I forecast a very fulfilling relationship for us, Chloe Lawrence.'

She stepped back, smiling, her hair outlined in an aureole of fire from the light behind her. 'I think you're right,' she said demurely, and looked up as the clock in the church tower struck one. 'It's late. And will be later by the time you get to Clieve House.'

'And cold.' He grinned. 'I wonder if Mrs Scott's got a spare hot-water bottle?'

Chloe giggled. 'I could lend you mine,' she offered.

'Not red socks *and* a hot-water bottle?'

'You don't live in a house like this one!'

He gave a crow of laughter. 'Think of the effect on your admirers if I leaked that bit of news.'

'If it rules out incidents of the Tim Armstrong genre, go ahead,' she said, unmoved.

His eyes lit with something which took her breath away. 'The only effect it has on me, Chloe, is a burning desire to take the hot-water bottle's place in your bed. Goodnight.'

Chloe watched him set off at a pace designed to conquer the cold, then turned back into the house, smiling dreamily until certain sounds pierced her reverie. She ran to the kitchen to find her mother had almost finished washing-up.

'Gwen, what are you doing!'

'Won't take a minute, darling—and I certainly didn't expect you to ask Piers Audley to help with the dishes.'

Chloe grinned as she wielded a teatowel. 'It never occurred to him to offer! I expect he's got a dishwasher in his flat, or someone who comes in to deal with the practicalities of life.'

'Does he live alone?' enquired Gwen casually.

'Yes he does, and before you ask there's apparently no woman in his life at present, though there have been in the past, and we had a very nice evening, and no, he hasn't made any arrangements to see me again—but just wait until I tell you what he has in mind for Clieve House!'

At least, thought Chloe in bed later, she didn't *think* Piers had said anything definite about another meeting.

His plans had all been for the future, rather than immediate. And after such a demanding evening, she tried to convince herself, a Sunday spent doing nothing at all was probably a very good thing before she plunged back into the cut and thrust of life at Propax Pharmaceuticals.

She found it hard to sleep. The brief, stormy interludes of lovemaking during the evening had left her body in a state of tension new to it. At the thought of Piers's mouth and caressing hands her stomach muscles clenched and her breathing quickened and she was obliged to thump and turn her pillows and make yet another attempt to settle down for the night. Then at last, when she was finally beginning to feel drowsy, a different face swam into her mind, with accusing eyes full of reproach.

Go away, she ordered it sharply. You'll soon be married to someone else. Leave me in peace!

Expecting to lie awake all night, Chloe found she'd slept half the morning through before her mother burst into the room to wake her, excitement on her pretty, round face.

'Chloe, wake up, you dormouse. Piers has just rung.'

Chloe peered at her mother, then gave a great yawn. 'What did he want?' she asked sleepily.

'He wants to take us both out to lunch today.' Gwen eyed her daughter expectantly. 'I said yes. I hope I did the right thing.'

Chloe sat up, thrusting her hair out of her eyes as she realised it was just what she'd been hoping for. She smiled happily at her mother. 'You always do the right thing—*and* you deserve a break from the Sunday roast!'

CHAPTER SEVEN

THE weekend of Piers's fateful visit to Little Compton marked a watershed in Chloe's life. From then on he left her in no doubt that he meant what he said about seeing as much of her as circumstances allowed. Jessica was agog when she found Piers Audley was not only making regular visits to Clieve House to oversee its conversion, but spending every available minute with Chloe each time he was there.

'Are his intentions honourable?' she demanded one Sunday, on her own for once while David spent a weekend with his parents.

The two girls were lingering over breakfast while Gwen was at church, the dogs close to the Aga to enjoy the delicious scents of roasting beef coming from the oven.

'We're just—friends,' said Chloe demurely, then laughed at the look in her sister's eyes.

'And I'm the Queen of Sheba. Come off it, Chloe.' Jessica grinned. 'It was quite obvious on New Year's Eve that the man was taken with you—David surprised you *in flagrante* with him, remember, that same action-packed night.'

'It was a kiss, not *flagrante*,' retorted Chloe, but Jessica wasn't having any.

'Have you slept with him?' she demanded.

'No, I have not!' howled Chloe, incensed. 'And even if I had, I wouldn't tell you.'

'All right, keep that red hair on. Though why you haven't, I can't imagine,' said her sister frankly. 'When do you see him again?'

'I was coming to that,' said Chloe, getting up to make coffee. 'Could I possibly bag your sofabed next weekend? Piers has invited me to some thrash given by his head of chambers. He offered to book a room for me at a hotel, but it seems a waste with you to hand in Ealing.'

Jessica eyed Chloe thoughtfully. 'He's invited you to his chambers? Isn't that a bit—well, significant?'

'I don't know. Is it?'

'Does he have a mother?'

'No. Parents dead, and no siblings, lucky chap.' Chloe smiled to soften the last, then eyed Jessica's calculating face with suspicion. 'Now what?'

'Well, don't you see, idiot? Parading you before his chums and colleagues is the next best thing to taking you home to mother. The man,' added Jessica dramatically, 'means business!'

'Rubbish,' said Chloe uneasily. 'Why does everybody bang on about marriage all the time? Gwen's just as bad.'

'Understandable, snookums.' Jess smiled lovingly. 'To our darling Gwen he's a lot more eligible than Mick Streeter.'

Chloe grinned. 'Not many mothers would turn their nose up at Mick's earning capacity.'

'Ah, but it comes with a pony-tail and a reluctance to shave, not to mention a very odd taste in clothes and jewellery.'

'Mick's a good man. I'm very fond of him——'

'Never mind him, let's keep to the present candidate, who probably shaves twice a day and patronises Savile Row for his clothes.' Jess fixed Chloe with a quizzical eye. 'Why do you want to stay at my place? Surely Piers would have preferred you with him.'

'I'm not quite ready for that. Yet.'

'Do you mean you don't fancy him that way?'

'As a matter of fact, I do——' Chloe jumped up restlessly. 'But it's much too early in the day for this kind of discussion. Time I did the vegetables.'

Not for the world would Chloe have let on that she was like a cat on hot bricks at the thought of the party at Piers's chambers. The very words 'Middle Temple' were daunting enough. The prospect of introduction to Piers Audley's colleagues and their wives, some of the latter also barristers, and all of them at home in such esoteric legal circles, filled Chloe with foreboding. Which, she told herself crossly, was utterly stupid. In the past she'd strutted down catwalks in London, Paris and Rome without turning a hair, and talked nonsense with a glass of champagne in her hand at parties without number. She'd taken it all in her stride, Mick's tutelage engendering more confidence with every occasion, to the point where she could exchange badinage with the best. Because all that had been a part she was playing, nothing to do with the real Chloe. Yet now, even with the modelling in her past and the more sober success of her present job to bolster her up, she had the jitters.

When Piers had first mentioned the party Chloe had assumed her navy satin dress would do. When he told her it was a midday drinks party she was floored. Her daytime clothes were geared strictly to severe business suits for her job. There was no snappy little number in her wardrobe remotely suitable for this particular occasion.

'I don't know what to wear,' she blurted to Piers when he rang her up two days before the event.

He hooted with laughter. 'Can this be the celebrated model talking? You look wonderful in anything, Chloe. As I,' he added, with meaning, 'know better than most. I speak of the socks.'

'Will you shut up about those socks?' she said impatiently. 'What kind of things will the other women be wearing?'

'I've no idea. What does it matter?'

'A typically male statement!'

'I'll be glad to see you whatever you're wearing. I miss you,' he said abruptly, changing the subject. 'Tell me you miss me.'

Chloe blinked. 'I do,' she admitted breathlessly. 'Rather a lot.'

He let out an audible hiss of breath. 'Don't tell me things like that over the phone, it's bad for my blood-pressure. What time will you arrive on Saturday morning? I'll meet your train.'

'Actually I'm travelling up tomorrow night——'

'Hell, Chloe, I'm tied up then with a circuit dinner!'

'I know. You told me. I'll be late, anyway. I've got to get home from Pennington first. Then Gwen's driving me to the station and I'll go straight to Jessica's.'

'No travelling by Tube at that time of night,' he ordered. 'Take a taxi.'

'I don't go into London at all. I change at Reading and get a train direct to West Ealing.'

'You'll still need a taxi. Leave a message on my answering machine when you get to your sister's flat.'

'Yes, sir, certainly, sir.'

'Would that you were always as compliant,' he said drily.

'I'm coming to your party,' she pointed out.

'Does that mean you'd rather not?'

'No. Not exactly. I just hope I won't feel like a fish out of water among you legal eagles.'

He laughed. 'You're mixing metaphors! But you won't feel out of place, I promise. And take heart. These things don't last long. We should be in reasonable time to make it for a hotpot at Simpsons-in-the-Strand afterwards. Shall I drive to Ealing to pick you up?'

'No, don't do that, I'll get a cab. I'll meet you at your chambers about twelve on Saturday, then.'

'Come earlier than that. And make sure you find my room first. I want you to myself for a while before the others come. And Chloe,' he added, 'indulge me, please. Leave your hair down.'

Chloe took a long lunch hour next day to search for something suitable for the occasion. Consoling herself it would do very well for Jessica's wedding afterwards, she splashed out on a severe, wildly expensive dress and matching coat in pin-striped brown linen. While her reckless mood lasted she added fawn suede shoes and bag fashioned by some master Italian hand, then sprinted back to the office out of breath and out of pocket.

'You can't go on the Underground in that,' said Jessica, blenching at the price ticket later that night.

'Why not?' said Chloe. 'It's a serviceable colour, and the dress is actually stretch linen so it shouldn't crease too much.'

'If it's coming to my wedding it's not going on the Tube,' said Jess firmly. 'I'm meeting David at his place for lunch with his best man tomorrow. I'll drive you that far, then you can take a taxi the rest of the way.'

Chloe was glad she'd given in next morning when she was ready. The brown pinstripes were so flattering, even to her own eyes, she felt reluctant to expose them to public transport. Following Piers's instructions she left her hair down, brushing it until it gleamed like russet satin before securing it at the nape of her neck with the gilt and tortoiseshell butterfly clasp she kept for special occasions.

'What do you think?' she asked Jessica when she was ready. 'Too much make-up?'

'Absolutely not. You look fantastic! But no jewellery?' added Jessica, surprised.

'I lost one of my glass hearts so I thought I'd just stick to my butterfly.' Chloe craned to see her back view in the mirror. 'You don't think it looks a bit ornate for this time of day?'

'What's the matter with you, girl? Of course it doesn't—and normally you'd know that perfectly well.' Jessica grinned. 'Piers Audley's opinion obviously matters quite a lot.'

Chloe met her sister's sparkling brown eyes in the mirror. 'In this particular instance it certainly does. I haven't met any of his friends before.'

'You look perfect, so stop dithering.' Jessica removed a long, curling red hair from Chloe's shoulder. 'If you don't come back tonight I won't mind,' she said casually.

'Why? Is David coming round?'

'No, it's his weekend on call so I'm going to his place. And Monica's away for the weekend, so you can bring your lawman back for coffee or even not come back at all. It's up to you.'

'How liberal of you, sister dear! But the coffee bit sounds more likely.' Chloe glanced at her watch. 'Right. I don't want to rush you, but if you're ready——'

By the time her taxi was speeding along the Embankment butterflies were running riot in Chloe's

middle regions. When they arrived she paid the driver,
then made for the forbidding façade of the eighteenth-
century building which housed Piers Audley's chambers.
She glanced at her watch, not at all pleased to find she
was earlier than she'd have liked as she went through
the swing doors into a narrow stone hallway. Glad her
destination was on the fourth floor, she ignored the lift
and set off up the worn stone steps to fill in time.
Eventually, dawdling as long as possible over the climb,
she arrived at a half-open door with a list of barristers'
names in white paint, Piers Audley's near the top.

Chloe studied it, impressed, then turned the handle
of the inner door to find herself in a long passage with
a red carpet and carved upright chairs, the walls lined
with bookshelves interspersed with spaces hung with an-
tique sporting prints. Ahead of her the door she was
looking for stood half open. She knocked on it, then
when no one answered went inside to wait, as Piers had
instructed. It was an unexpectedly peaceful room,
smelling of paper and leather and polish, with a gleaming
parquet floor only partially covered by a thin, beautiful
carpet obviously woven a long time ago in some part of
Persia. Like the corridor, the walls were given over
mainly to books, with heavy velvet curtains framing
views of the gardens on one side, the Middle Temple
spire on the other. In one half of the room stood a large,
leather-topped desk; the other half was dominated by a
huge, battered table heaped with paper bundles tied with
pink tapes.

She whirled round as the door closed with a click, and
there stood Piers, heavy fair hair gleaming, and so
dauntingly elegant for a split second he seemed like a
stranger. Then she met amber eyes alight with welcome

and something else which caught at Chloe's vitals like a clutching hand.

'You're on time.' He strode across the room, taking her in his arms to hold her close, his lips against her cheek. 'I want to kiss your mouth——'

'If you do,' she warned breathlessly, 'you'll wreck a good morning's work.'

He smoothed his cheek against hers then stood back to scrutinise her at leisure. 'Are you telling me it took a long time to produce such ravishingly simple perfection?'

'Longer than usual, anyway!' Chloe pivoted in a slow, practised circle. 'Well?'

Piers looked at her for a moment, heavy lids dropping like shutters to conceal the heat of his response. 'Flawless—straight off the cover of *Vogue*.'

She made a face. 'Sounds a bit cold and inhuman.'

'Good. If that's the impression you give my male colleagues I'll be deeply grateful. I haven't forgotten New Year's Eve,' he said with feeling.

'Neither have I.'

Their eyes met.

'Certain aspects of it are etched indelibly in my mind,' said Piers, the drawl very much in evidence.

'If you're talking about those socks again, I'll scream,' she told him, smiling.

'As it happens, I wasn't.' His eyes fell to her mouth and she bit her lip. 'If you do that,' he growled, 'I'll be forced to kiss it better.'

Voices outside broke the thread of sexual tension between them, and Piers smiled.

'People are starting to arrive. We'll continue this conversation later.' He waved a hand at her clothes. 'I assume this is new?'

'Yes. I had a madly extravagant lunch hour yesterday.'

He frowned. 'I hope you're not out of pocket over a few drinks at chambers, Chloe.'

'Don't worry, I'm wearing it to Jessica's wedding, too.' She moved over to the window to look out.

Piers moved to stand close behind her, his arms coming round to clasp her waist. 'You're not a bridesmaid, then?'

'Heavens, no.' She gave a brittle laugh. 'Jess just wants a quiet, family affair. Lisa's the one set on the wedding of the year.'

'Your services as bridesmaid not required there, either?'

Chloe turned in the circle of his arms to look him in the eye. 'Even in lowish heels I'm five feet ten. Lisa is five foot nothing, several pounds heavier than she admits to, and haunted by the spectre of Chloe the model. She couldn't hide her relief when I suggested she stick with a brace of small nieces instead.'

'Would you like a conventional wedding, Chloe?'

She broke free to turn to the window again. 'That's a pretty tactless question.'

'It wasn't meant to be. Most girls dream of drifting down the aisle in a cloud of white lace or whatever.'

'For obvious reasons, I do not,' she said flatly. She went over to the desk and took a mirror from her bag, studied her face then renewed her lipstick. 'Well?' she said challengingly to the man watching her. 'Is it time to join the others?'

To Chloe's surprise she enjoyed the party very much. From the moment Piers introduced her to Gervase Marriott, his head of chambers, all the qualms of the morning disappeared, leaving her feeling rather foolish that she'd ever had any. She felt relaxed almost at once, her smile warm as she responded to the formal charm of the eminent Queen's Counsel. Gervase, as she was bidden to call him, was a balding, beak-nosed man with lazy, clever eyes. He presented his wife, Hester, a brisk, friendly woman who took Chloe under her wing and made the rounds of the other barristers of both sexes, along with their assorted partners, a process which had Chloe's head reeling after the first half-dozen names. Not that she need have worried. Piers stayed close as his colleagues vied with each other for the attention of the guest one man termed as 'our eligible Audley's delightful friend'.

'This is Simon Chandler,' said Piers. 'I was his pupilmaster not long ago, but I doubt he benefited from the experience.'

'If you mean I don't earn as much money as you, Piers, you're damn right,' said the young man, taking Chloe's hand. Simon Chandler was tall enough to tower over Chloe, a novel experience for her as she smiled up into laughing dark eyes beneath black hair which flopped in a glossy wing over his forehead. As she returned his greeting Simon frowned. 'Haven't we met somewhere?'

'Lord, Chandler, if you can't think of something more original than that,' said Piers in mock sorrow, 'my teachings were definitely all in vain.'

In response to a signal from Gervase Marriott, Piers made Chloe a swift apology and left her with Simon and a couple of other young men only too eager to make her acquaintance. For a while she was the centre of an animated group all vying for her attention until suddenly Simon snapped his fingers, his face bright with triumph.

'I know where I've seen you!' he told Chloe. 'I thought your name rang a bell. My sister once yearned to be a model and she cut pictures of her favourites out of magazines. Your face took pride of place on her bedroom wall!'

At once there was such hubbub among the group that Piers came over to investigate, putting a possessive arm round Chloe's waist.

'This rabble bothering you?' he demanded, fixing the young men with a cold, gleaming eye.

'Not really,' she said, smiling. 'They discovered my guilty secret, that's all. One of them at least,' she added lightly, flushing a little as Piers gave her a sudden, narrowed look.

'Is it safe to leave you with this lot while I talk shop with Gervase just five minutes longer?' asked Piers in an undertone.

'Of course.' Chloe smiled at him. 'I'll wave if I need help.'

When she turned back to the others she found that Simon, by some practised bit of trickery, had managed to cut out the other two young men so he could have her to himself in one corner of the impressive, panelled room.

'Have you known Piers long?' he asked, standing as close as he dared.

Chloe moved back a little, giving him the practised smile she'd once employed in hundreds of similar situations. 'Not very long.'

'I haven't seen your face lately. Have you given up modelling?'

'I retired from it years ago.'

'But you're still younger than me! Wasn't that early to give it all up? Sorry to be nosey, but Caroline will be agog when she hears I met you.'

'I just wanted a different type of career,' said Chloe with complete truth, aware that Piers was watching them from across the room.

Simon Chandler went on to fire questions at her, asking where she lived, if she came up to town often, whether she'd care to dine with him some time when she did. Chloe fended him off expertly, smiling at him because despite his rather brash self-confidence Simon was a born charmer, and took all her smiling refusals in his stride with no hint of animosity when she made it plain she was unavailable.

'Right then, darling,' said a familiar voice, with a certain tone to it which alerted Chloe to Piers's displeasure. 'I don't know how this ruffian managed to get you to himself, but it's time you circulated, young Chandler. Mrs Marriott is fixing you with her eye.'

Simon sprang to attention. 'Yes sir, Mr Audley sir, on my way.' He smiled at Chloe. 'See you again before you go.'

'You made quite an impression on him,' remarked Piers acidly.

'Only because he recognised my face,' Chloe said calmly. 'Besides, he's a very charming young man.'

'And noted for chasing anything in a skirt,' he snapped.

'Why, thank you,' said Chloe, in a voice as sweet and cold as ice-cream. 'That certainly puts me in my place.'

Piers took her hand in a crushing grip, baulked from saying anything more as Hester Marriott joined them with two people who'd just arrived, a thin, dark man with a smile of great charm, and a vivid blonde with a white cashmere coat slung over her shoulders, pearls cascading down a blue wool dress which clung to every ripe curve of her figure.

Her pinstripes suddenly reduced to all the allure of a school uniform, Chloe guessed the identity of the woman long before Piers made the introduction.

'Chloe, meet Maxine Grierson, and her husband Rupert, who rules over the chambers on the ground floor. This is Miss Chloe Lawrence,' he added with a proprietorial air as she made the usual conventional murmurs.

'And are you anything to do with the law, Miss Lawrence?' asked Rupert Grierson, smiling warmly.

'Nothing at all,' she assured him.

'Yet I'm certain we've met somewhere,' said Maxine, frowning. 'You look very familiar.'

'*Et tu, Brute.*' Piers glanced down at Chloe's resigned face. 'If you subscribe to various glossy magazines you've probably seen pictures of her enough in the past.'

'You're a model!' said Rupert, delighted. 'I've never met one before.'

Maxine snapped her fingers. 'That's it, of course! But I've seen you on television more. You washed that gorgeous red hair in a stream then threw it back from your face and looked so slender and ravishing I detested you. I was pregnant and barrel-shaped at the time,' she explained, laughing.

Chloe joined in the laughter as Piers slid an arm round her waist. 'I detested that one myself. I thought I'd freeze to death.'

'I wish I'd known,' said Maxine with feeling, 'I wouldn't have felt so envious. But I seem to remember something with a leopard, too.'

'A leopard!' said the men simultaneously.

Chloe nodded. 'It was a stocking advertisement. The leopard appeared to rub itself against my legs, but it was trick photography, I'm happy to say.' She smiled. 'I gave it all up years ago. I work for a pharmaceutical company these days.'

'Really? But my dear, what on earth do you *do* there?' said Maxine in astonishment.

Piers smiled down at Chloe. 'At the moment she's the woman behind the marketing director's throne, but who knows? One day she might be chairman of the company.'

'I seriously doubt that,' laughed Chloe, grateful to Piers, but in no way put out by Maxine Grierson's curiosity. As they talked together for a few minutes longer it was very obvious that Rupert Grierson and his wife shared an enviable rapport.

A few minutes later Piers relieved Chloe of her glass and said it was time to go.

'Piers tells me you live in Gloucestershire, Chloe,' said Maxine, as they said goodbye. 'When you come up next Piers must bring you to dinner. You can meet my gorgeous sons.'

'Holy terrors, you mean!' Rupert gave a rather smug smile to his wife. 'Why not broadcast the news, darling?'

Maxine nodded happily. 'He means there's a third holy terror in the offing at the end of the summer.'

'And to think you were once the brightest pupil Gervase ever had!' said Piers and kissed the blooming cheek she presented to him.

'I much prefer my present occupation,' she said serenely.

'Congratulations,' said Chloe with sincerity. 'Motherhood obviously suits you.'

Maxine smiled, delighted. 'I strongly recommend it!'

Piers detached Chloe at once. 'Time we were off.' They made the rounds of the room, then thanked Gervase and Hester Marriott, and were about to leave when Simon

Chandler came sprinting across the room to take leave of Chloe.

'I meant what I said,' he assured her, his eyes dancing at the look Piers stabbed at him. 'Any time you're at a loose end when you're in town, ring me. I'm in the book.'

'What the hell did he mean by that?' demanded Piers when they gained the relative calm of the hall.

'Nothing very much,' returned Chloe shortly. 'It's the sort of thing men always say at parties.'

'Is that one in the eye for me?'

She shook her head. 'Not at all. Where there are parties there are people like Simon Chandler. Perfectly harmless. Especially,' she added, 'as my trips to London can hardly be described as frequent.'

'If they were would you get in touch with him?'

Chloe gave him a disdainful glare.

'The lift's a bit dodgy,' said Piers, eyeing her warily. 'Shall we go down the stairs?'

'By all means. That's the way I came up.'

In silence they descended the smooth, worn stone steps, constraint heavy in the air between them. The day outside was bright with spring sunshine as they made for the car, but the atmosphere inside it was arctic as Chloe fastened her seatbelt.

'What's the matter?' asked Piers, getting in beside her. 'I've obviously made you angry.'

'Any woman would be angry classified as something in a skirt, Piers Audley!'

'I put it crudely. I apologise. It just got me on the raw to see that young puppy monopolising you. Particularly since you seemed perfectly happy about it.'

'It was a party at your chambers,' she reminded him. 'I could hardly walk away and cause a scene.'

'You could have looked less delighted by my absence!'

Chloe gave him a fulminating look. 'You could have warned me we might meet your beautiful Maxine, too.'

'Was that a problem for you?' he said instantly, his normal aplomb suddenly firmly in place.

'No. I liked her.'

'But I suppose you get tired of all the "haven't we met before" line.'

'Just a little.' Chloe yawned suddenly as Piers started the car.

'Bored?' he demanded.

'Strain,' she said tersely.

'You weren't really nervous about meeting that crowd, were you?'

'I was beforehand,' she admitted. 'Actually they were all very charming. I enjoyed it.'

'Particularly the exchange with young Chandler, I take it!'

Chloe kept a haughty silence, unwilling to let Piers know her enjoyment had come to a very sudden end at the last, when Maxine Grierson had announced she was pregnant. Chloe was no stranger to the stab of envy which pierced her; the knowledge that motherhood was unlikely to be something she'd experience herself was nothing new. But every fresh reminder acted like salt on a raw wound, just the same.

CHAPTER EIGHT

'You look pale,' commented Piers. 'Perhaps it might be as well to alter the plan a little. We could take pot luck at my place for lunch, then afterwards you can relax for a while and we'll go out to dinner tonight.'

Chloe nodded distantly, not at all keen to lunch at a restaurant with the present air of constraint hanging over them. 'Thank you. I'd prefer that. I really don't think I could face a restaurant at the moment, but a snack of some kind wouldn't come amiss. I was too nervous to eat breakfast.'

'Which was hardly sensible,' said Piers in disapproval. 'Luckily we haven't far to go.'

His home, Chloe found, was a Georgian house of great charm in the Gray's Inn Road. She eyed it, impressed, as they arrived. Piers Audley had to be earning very good money indeed to afford an establishment of this kind.

'It belonged to my parents,' he informed her, apparently reading her mind as he conducted her through rooms furnished in a style reminiscent of his chambers, with a sparse taste which appealed strongly to Chloe.

'This is lovely,' she said politely. 'Not in the least like the Parsonage, yet just as welcoming. Odd, really. The two houses could hardly be less alike.'

'When I inherited the place it seemed only sensible to keep it on owing to its proximity to the Temple. It's too big for one, of course,' he added, and shrugged wryly. 'I always assumed I'd marry one day and fill it with children.'

He opened a door into a room which was obviously his study. 'This is my retreat. I spend most of my time in here.'

'I can see that.' Chloe eyed more book-lined walls, a massive desk and very masculine leather furniture. A complicated stereo system occupied some of the shelves, and a television stood in one corner.

'I never have much time to watch that,' he said, following her gaze. 'I tend to bring a lot of work home.'

'Who looks after you?' she asked.

'A very efficient lady comes in during the week to keep the place in shape, and does the basic shopping for me. On the catering side I generally eat out or get something sent in. Talking of which,' he added, 'come to the kitchen and see what we can find.' He halted halfway across the hall. 'Are you still cold?'

'I'm afraid so.'

'The heating's going full blast, so it must be nerves. I'll find a sweater for you.' Piers smiled faintly. 'Length won't be a problem, but otherwise you'll be swamped.'

They ate lunch in Piers's kitchen, which, unlike the rest of the house, was very modern and streamlined. Chloe was glad of her borrowed sweater, which was several sizes too large, but a welcome addition to the sleeveless dress. After a little canned consommé laced with sherry, plus bread and cheese and some polite remarks about the house, Chloe felt better.

'I feel more human now,' she said, as she sipped her coffee.

'You haven't eaten much.' Piers eyed her searchingly. 'Was it really such an ordeal?'

'No. I liked it.'

'Particularly the episode with Simon Chandler, I take it.'

'Are you going to keep on about that all day? If so I'll take the next train back home.'

He stared at her moodily. 'It was a new experience for me.'

Her eyes narrowed. 'What was?'

'Jealousy.'

'That's stupid.'

'You don't have to tell me that!' he snapped, then looked at her in silence for a while. 'I want you to come to more parties like that in the future.'

Chloe shrugged non-committally. 'I don't come up to London very often.'

'That must change,' he said flatly. 'Once Clieve House is fully operational I'll have nowhere to stay in Little Compton unless I put up at a hotel every time I come to see you.'

She stirred her coffee thoughtfully. 'But if I ask you to stay at the Parsonage——'

'Your mother and brother will be demanding my intentions,' he finished for her. 'I saw Marcus in action with young Armstrong, remember. It's pretty obvious he feels very protective where you're concerned.'

'Interfering, you mean.'

'Doesn't he live in London, too?'

'Yes, in Barnes.'

'Are you going to see him this weekend?'

'No. I haven't even told him I'm coming up.' She yawned again suddenly, then apologised, embarrassed. 'Sorry. I didn't sleep much last night.'

'Then make up for it now. If I show you up to one of the guest-rooms, why not take a rest?' He raised a sardonic eyebrow. 'Alone, of course, Chloe.'

'I didn't dream otherwise,' she said briskly, and got up. 'I'd better take advantage of the offer, otherwise I'll be very poor company for the rest of the day.'

'I doubt that, Chloe.' Piers led the way upstairs to a quiet, restful room, pointed out the adjoining bathroom, then left her alone.

Chloe undressed down to her brief silk slip, then went into the bathroom to remove all traces of the make-up she'd applied with such care earlier in the day. She unfastened the clasp in her hair, ran her fingers through the crackling, fiery strands, then climbed into the wide, welcoming bed with a sigh. She smiled wryly at the ceiling, certain that Jess, along with everyone at the Marriotts' party, would find it hard to believe she was in bed in Piers Audley's guest-room while he stayed downstairs alone. But love in the afternoon had never been on the agenda, she knew very well. Despite his mood earlier she felt very much in tune with Piers. And deeply gratified by his jealousy, if she were honest. In fact, she realised drowsily, other than the obvious exception the only man she'd ever shared anything like such rapport with before was Mick. And he didn't count.

Chloe slept deeply, hardly moving a muscle in the comfortable bed. She lay motionless, unaware that Piers, coming to check on her at one stage, frowned and touched her outflung hand, checking the pulse in her blue-veined wrist.

When she finally woke up Chloe yawned widely then looked at her watch in consternation to find she'd been fast asleep for the best part of four hours. Before she could get out of bed there was a quiet tap on the door and Piers came in, wearing a dark blue track suit.

'You're awake.' He closed the door behind him and strolled round the side of the bed. 'Do you feel better?'

She nodded drowsily. 'Much better.' She eyed his clothes curiously. 'What have you been doing?'

'A spot of rowing—in my bathroom. A gesture at keeping fit.' He smiled and touched a hand to her hair. 'You look rested, Chloe.'

She stretched luxuriously under the covers. 'I feel quite wonderful.'

'As wonderful as you look?'

Chloe felt a surge of response to the intimacy of his tone. She saw his tawny irises darken, felt her heart beat faster, and bit her lip. Then remembered, too late.

'I told you what would happen if you did that,' he warned, and sat down on the bed and pulled her warm, pliant body up into his arms to kiss her long and hard. He raised his head to look deep into her dilated eyes. 'I promised myself I wouldn't do that. At least not here, not now.'

Chloe smiled slowly, in a way which tightened his arms round her. 'Is all this because I smiled and exchanged party chit-chat with another man?'

'Partly. I even wanted to thump the conceited young puppy.' He breathed in deeply and kissed her again, his muscles tightening as she slid her hands up over his shoulders to lock them behind his neck. He took his lips from hers with effort, looking her in the eye as her hands slid away. 'You'll want to dress. I'd better get out of here—while I still can.'

'Please stay,' Chloe blurted, to her own astonishment.

Piers laid her very deliberately back against the pillows. 'Why?' he demanded.

She glared at him. 'Isn't it obvious?'

'Not where you're concerned, Chloe.' He leaned over her, one hand playing with a lock of her hair. 'If I stay here even one minute longer I'll make love to you. Is that what you're inviting? Because I warn you, Chloe, I'm not used to keeping myself on such a tight rein. I want you, as must be perfectly obvious. And I'm willing to wait until you want me even a fraction as much, but this isn't fair.'

Chloe gazed up at him, unblinking, a smile playing at the corners of her mouth. 'The minute's up.'

A light blazed in his eyes, as though someone had flipped a switch, then he stretched out on the bed beside her, holding her so close their mingled, accelerated heartbeat reverberated through both of them with a force which took Chloe's breath away.

'There's something you ought to know,' she said, panicking.

'If you mean you'd rather I was someone else at this juncture,' he said grimly, 'I'd rather not hear.'

'No, no, you don't understand!' said Chloe urgently, and felt some of the tension leave him as he slackened his hold.

'Enlighten me,' he ordered.

'You'll laugh.' She burrowed her face against him.

Piers put a finger under her chin and raised her face to his. 'I'm more likely to explode if you don't tell me!'

'It's just—well—I've never done this before,' she muttered, and coloured hectically at the incredulity in his eyes.

Piers lay very still for a moment, then he sat up, pushed the pillows up against the carved headboard and drew her into his arms so that she lay cradled against his shoulder like a child. 'My darling girl,' he said, in a tone so uncharacteristically tender that her stomach muscles contracted. 'Since it's obvious you're telling me the truth——'

'I'd be a fool to lie, wouldn't I!' she snapped, stiffening.

He ran a gentling hand down the silk covering her spine. 'It's just so hard to believe.' He frowned. 'But why, Chloe? As you've said yourself there were plenty of men in your life in your modelling days, not to mention the relationship with your photographer friend.'

'It's perfectly simple. I never wanted to sleep with any of them, so I didn't.' Chloe smiled wryly. 'And not one of those likely lads was ever going to admit he hadn't scored with Chloe Lawrence, now, was he! Thus are legends born. And Mick——' She hesitated. 'Off the record, Mick's not interested in girls in that way. But he's the best friend I've ever had, just the same.'

'Which explains a lot,' said Piers, enlightened.

Chloe nodded. 'Mick got the chance to make it in the States about the time I went back to college, so we haven't seen much of each other since. But he usually looks me up when he's in the UK.'

Piers held her closer, rubbing his cheek over her hair. 'But apart from all that I suppose the real, basic reason for your celibacy is obvious.'

'Exactly. To you, anyway. If I couldn't have the man I wanted I couldn't bear the thought of anyone else.' Chloe sighed. 'I lived in a sort of emotional glass case.'

'So why are you opening up to me?'

She looked up at him very directly. 'I met you at the exact moment the official engagement became a kind of stop sign in my life, warning me to face reality. And you altered my entire sexual outlook. Up to then I'd had this fairy-tale idea that for me, personally, involvement of the heart was essential for a physical relationship with a man.'

His arms tightened. 'And now?'

She touched a hand to his cheek. 'Now I know differently. *You've* taught me that, and I suppose things developed between us far more quickly than usual because of the greenhouse effect of New Year's Eve. I confess I hated sharing my pathetic secret with you at first, sure it would be a barrier between us. But oddly enough it's the reverse. I like not having to pretend with you.' She gave him the luminous smile which had once brought her such success in front of the camera. 'In short, Piers Audley, you're the only other man in my life I've ever had the least desire to make love with——'

The last words were lost against his lips as he kissed her hard in response to her admission. 'You've waited long enough to tell me that,' he said huskily, and gazed down into her face for so long Chloe grew restless.

'What is it?'

'Is your sister expecting you back tonight?'

'Not if I don't want to go.' Chloe looked away. 'She's staying with David.'

'To hell with *David*!' said Piers with sudden savagery. He released her suddenly and leapt to his feet.

Chloe stared at him in disbelief. 'It's a bit deflating to be turned down after all those girlish revelations, Piers Audley!'

He grasped her shoulders, drawing her up to her knees to kiss her until her head reeled. 'I'm doing nothing of the kind,' he said against her parted mouth. 'But in the light of those same revelations, let's rewrite the scenario, Chloe.'

Her eyes gleamed with speculation. 'What exactly do you have in mind?'

He smiled very slowly, trailing a fingertip down her cheek. 'I suggest we drive to your sister's flat, collect your belongings, have dinner somewhere on the way back then continue this particular conversation at leisure.' He raised an eyebrow. 'Does the programme appeal?'

'Very much,' she said demurely, and smiled at him.

'Then get dressed and downstairs in twenty minutes,' he commanded and strode from the room with a suspicion of a swagger Chloe found strangely endearing.

She slid out of bed and made for the bathroom to stand under the shower with a towel wrapped round her hair. She dressed hurriedly, did her face with skilful speed, then brushed her crackling, curling hair loose and flew downstairs to meet Piers's countdown with only a few seconds to spare. As they drove through the fine spring evening Chloe chattered to Piers about her working week, fired questions at him about his, and, far from being tense with nerves about the night ahead, anticipation of it gave her face a lustre Piers remarked on with some amusement.

'An afternoon nap is obviously worth more than all the cosmetics in Harrods.'

'Was I such a hag for the party, then?'

'As you know perfectly well, you outshone every woman there.'

'Not Maxine Grierson.' Chloe eyed him challengingly. 'You didn't tell me she was so beautiful.'

'She was less so when I knew her.' The corners of Piers's mouth went down. 'At that time she was totally career-minded, and her looks reflected that—determined and clearcut rather than beautiful. Now she's Mother Earth personified.'

'Full marks to Rupert Grierson, then.'

'Yes—very bad for my ego!' He shrugged as he took the turning she indicated.

'Did you ever propose marriage?'

'No. To Maxine or anyone else—is this the building?' He reached over to unfasten her seatbelt, brushing her cheek with his lips. 'I'll wait here. Don't be long.'

Chloe raced up the three flights of stairs to Jessica's flat, scribbled a note on the kitchen memo pad, then packed her bag and flew down to the waiting car again.

'You look very flushed. Having qualms?' he enquired as they drove off.

'No, of course not. It was my idea in the first place.' She scowled at Piers's sudden bark of laughter. 'What's so funny?'

'I wouldn't call it *your* idea, exactly. The idea of making love to you, Chloe Lawrence, took root the moment I set eyes on you—probably even before that, when I heard you sobbing behind the laurels.'

'How can you possibly have fancied someone who was crying her eyes out about another man?' demanded Chloe, astonished.

'My famed perception! Even without seeing her I could sense how seductive Niobe would be.'

'Actually I looked Niobe up and it doesn't apply at all, you know,' she informed him in schoolmarm fashion. 'She wasn't a maiden at all, she was grieving over her children.' She paused. 'Do you really think I'm seductive?'

'Don't ask leading questions,' said Piers flatly. 'You know damn well you are.'

Piers took her to dine at the Belvedere in Holland Park, where they ate onion tarts with sun-dried tomatoes and feta cheese, and a main dish of exquisitely prepared scallops. Afterwards Piers insisted Chloe try some of the restaurant's celebrated ice-cream for pudding, amused when she forgot to eat it in her excitement at seeing Elton John at one of the tables on the tier below.

'I expected you to be blasé about celebrities,' he commented over coffee. 'Surely Mick Streeter must have introduced you to a few in his time?'

She shook her head. 'He preferred to keep me separate from the rest of his life, so people would think we were actually lovers. Only you know for certain that we weren't, I think.' She smiled wryly. 'Another deadly secret for you to share.'

'I'm going to share more than that,' he said significantly.

Her eyes flew to meet his. 'Oh?'

He smiled slowly, the look in the intent amber eyes evoking the now familiar prickle of response along her spine. 'I'm going to marry you.'

They drove back to Gray's Inn Road in total silence, his words a tangible presence, like a third passenger in the car. When Piers finally closed his handsome front door on London they faced each other in his hall like boxers squaring up for a fight.

'Well?' he demanded. 'Surely you must have realised what I was building up to these past weeks?'

Chloe shook her head vigorously. 'No, I didn't. I thought you had something very different in mind.'

'Is the idea of marriage so far-fetched?' he challenged.

Chloe looked at the tall, autocratic figure in silence, thinking it over. 'No,' she said slowly after a while. 'Not far-fetched exactly. I'd just never considered the possibility. I knew you wanted us to be lovers. The thought of anything more permanent never occurred to me.'

'Then try thinking about it now,' said Piers briskly and ushered her into the study. 'Give me your coat, then curl up on the sofa. Drink?'

'No, thanks.' She pulled a face. 'I need a clear head for all this.'

Piers poured himself a small brandy and perched on the edge of his desk, loosening his silk tie. 'I'll outline the advantages. You say marriage is out for you due to your hankering after the wrong man. While for me you're the only woman I've ever wanted in my life on a permanent basis.'

She eyed him searchingly. 'So what's different about me?'

Piers gave a humourless laugh. 'If we knew the answer to that one, Chloe, we'd have solved the riddle of all human relationships. Physically I find you irresistible, as you well know, but it's not just that. I like being with you, and miss you when I'm not. It's as simple as that. I believe we could have a good life together, in bed and out of it. Neither of us expects the fabled grand passion that makes so many marriages come unstuck when it dies. We'd enter into the contract with eyes wide open.' He paused to drink some of the brandy, then looked at her with a wry smile. 'There's something else I should mention, too.'

'What is it?'

'When the Griersons made their announcement this morning I found, to my utter amazement, that I was envious.'

Chloe stared at him, arrested.

Piers frowned. 'Is it so strange that a man like me should want a child?'

'No, of course not.' She smiled a little. 'But it's strange that it happened to me at the same time. When Maxine gave us the glad news my biological clock gave a quite deafening chime in my ear.'

'It shouldn't have done, Chloe—you've got time to spare to produce a family.'

'Not without a very necessary form of assistance,' she pointed out. 'And with no prospect of a father for this unborn child I yearned for, not to mention your Othello act over Simon Chandler, I was not in the best of spirits when we left your chambers.'

'How very interesting.' Piers fixed her with a gleaming gold eye. 'Significant that we were struck simultaneously with the same thought, Chloe.'

'It's still not enough to rush us into something as important as marriage without a lot of hard thinking!'

'Then start up your thought processes as of now. I'm considered a good catch,' he said, with no trace of conceit. 'And for you, personally, my great advantage is my willingness to take on a bride in love with another man.'

'But doesn't that bother you?' she demanded, frowning.

He finished his brandy and set down the glass. 'No, because I refuse to think of it as an insurmountable obstacle. If anything it's a challenge.'

Chloe stared at him doubtfully, her mind in a whirl.

Piers closed the gap between them to stand over her, his smile telling her he scented victory. 'If your career is so important to you, Chloe, find a job here in London. Our lifestyle could easily support a nanny if that's what you'd prefer——'

'Hey!' Chloe held up a hand. 'Slow down. Let's ponder the marriage bit before any talk of nannies.'

'Or perhaps,' said Piers, with a sudden change of mood, 'there's something more important to consider even before that. Something which could influence your decision, one way or the other.' He held out his hands and she put hers into them, letting him pull her to her feet. 'I warn you I mean to use every power of persuasion I possess to make you say yes.'

Chloe looked at him thoughtfully. 'And if I say no?'

'But you won't,' he said, with supreme conviction. 'Listen, Chloe. Soon after meeting you my bachelor existence began to pall. And once I'd held you in my arms and felt your response to me I wanted you here with me all the time, sharing not only my bed but my life. One needn't be violently in love to feel a desire for companionship and marriage—and fatherhood.'

She thrust a hand through her hair, her eyes troubled. 'But, Piers, just because you've never been in love, it doesn't rule out the possibility in the future. You might fall in love quite hopelessly one day with some woman you've never laid eyes on up to now.'

'I can safely promise you that will never happen,' he said with certainty. 'And you'll have no extra-marital relationships to worry about where I'm concerned.' He looked at her levelly. 'Nor would I tolerate any from you.'

Chloe's eyes flashed coldly. 'I'd rather you hadn't felt it necessary to say that.'

'It's as well to make things clear from the start.'

'You make it sound more like a business transaction than a proposal!'

Piers promptly sank to one knee with grace, holding up his hand to her. 'Is that better?' he enquired drily, and Chloe laughed, her mood lightened.

'Oh, yes,' she assured him, 'and I'd feel better still if you got up and put your arms round me.'

'Ah, Chloe,' he said softly, leaping to his feet. 'I would have done from the first, but I thought you might think it smacked of coercion.'

'I think I fancy a little coercion at this juncture,' she whispered as he held her close. He laughed a little and kissed her gently, then not gently at all, with a fire she responded to with mounting excitement, returning the kiss with a fervour which made a statement of its own.

When Piers raised his head at last he was breathing rapidly, the light of conquest in his eyes. He took her by the hand and hurried her up the stairs, directing her past the room she'd slept in during the afternoon. 'This time I want you in my bed, where I've wanted you for weeks, with that hair of yours setting the pillows on fire.'

Later Chloe discovered that his room was typical of Piers, with nothing superfluous, the colours a combination of the subtle and sharp, in harmony with his personality. But for the moment she noticed nothing other than the feelings rising in her like champagne bubbles bursting to the surface, and she shivered as Piers laid her down on the bed.

'Nerves, Chloe?' he asked.

She smiled up at him as he hung over her.

'Some.'

'I won't hurt you, now or ever,' he promised, and bent to kiss her, then he turned her over and slid the zip open down the back of her dress and pulled it away, flinging it over a chair near the bed. Chloe heaved round and sat up, wreathing her arms round her knees as she smiled up at him.

'If that's how you're going to treat my cherished wardrobe I'll do the rest myself,' she said firmly and he laughed, sliding his hands from her ankles upwards in a caress which sent a great shiver through her.

'I promise I'll be more careful.' He smiled, then tensed, his breath catching as his fingers encountered smooth bare thigh. Lingering over the task, he peeled the stockings from her long, slender legs, then gazed down at her with a glittering hunger which started her heart beating like a drum. 'I think this is just about the stage where we called a halt this afternoon,' he said gruffly, and began to pull off his shirt.

She knelt up on the bed, restless with nervous anticipation. 'Let me give you a hand.'

'I want more than that, Chloe.' He threaded long fingers through her hair, tipping her face up to him. 'I want all of you.'

'Then stop talking and—and take what you want,' she said recklessly, an instruction which precipitated her flat on her back with Piers's hungry mouth on hers as he stripped off his clothes while he kissed her until her head reeled, a skill she registered with dazed admiration. When they lay together, naked at last in each other's arms, Chloe clenched teeth which chattered at the first touch of his body. Spare and hard and smooth for the most part, other areas were abrasive with hair which rasped against her skin, arousing sharply delicious sensations in her breasts; arrows of fire which shot from diamond-hard nipples to that part of her which thrust against him convulsively, then tensed in fright at contact with a rigid, velvet column of male need.

Piers held her close, and kissed her with reassuring tenderness, then smoothed her hair, his hands travelling lower over her spine, both gentling and arousing her as he turned her over to kiss the nape of her neck and the long curve of her spine. His mouth traced kisses over her buttocks and thighs, in the hollows of her knees and the delicate structure of her ankles, then she was on her back again and the caresses moved slowly upwards and she gasped as his fingers cajoled in subtle, caressing strokes from knee to thigh, until suddenly they breached the last of her defences and she gave a choked cry, writhing as his caresses brought her to the very edge of some hot, unimagined delight just out of reach.

Chloe's eyes opened on the intent, gold gaze above her. 'Now!' she said wildly, and raked her nails down his back, tearing away the last remnants of Piers's control as he complied with a convulsive thrust nothing like the gentle initiation he'd promised. She gave a sharp cry of pain and pushed upwards in instinctive desire to escape, only to impale herself further on the hard, throbbing flesh which held her captive.

Piers held her still, gentling her with caressing hands and whispered endearments as he subjugated his body to his will. Then slowly, almost imperceptibly, he began to move again. Chloe tensed against pain which never came. In its place there was only heat, and the new, unfamiliar sensation of possession. Her body began to move of its own volition in response, and she stared up into his face questioningly. She saw a leap of light in the tawny eyes as she gasped in surprise at the first throb of response. She undulated her hips instinctively to invite more and received it in full measure, the heat and sheer erotic pleasure of it taking her breath away as their bodies moved together in a compulsive rhythm which accelerated relentlessly, until Chloe's heart was hammering in her ears and she gasped for breath, her hair blinding both of them as her head tossed on the pillows and she clutched at his shoulders in entreaty. But to her dismay Piers suddenly buried his face in her neck with a stifled groan as his body convulsed and she was left, tantalised, denied the mysterious ecstasy experienced by her lover.

CHAPTER NINE

'THAT,' said Piers unevenly against her neck, 'doesn't usually happen.'

Chloe drew in a deep, unsteady breath. 'Which particular "that" are you referring to?'

'The last part.' He raised his head to look at her, dark colour along his cheekbones. 'You were so gloriously responsive that I lost control. Normally I pride myself on my ability to co-ordinate things rather better.'

Chloe frowned, and pushed her hair back from her damp forehead. 'I don't care much for the sound of that.'

'I'm not boasting. It's a statement of fact.'

'That's what I dislike about it. You sound so—so practised.'

He propped himself up on one elbow to look down at her. 'It would be unusual, Chloe, if I wasn't somewhat practised.'

She pulled a face. 'I suppose you've made love to hundreds of women.'

He gave a snort of laughter. 'Certainly not!' He smoothed a hand through her hair, disentangling it and teasing it out until it lay like a wine-red fan across the pillow. 'One-night stands have never been my style. I require more in common with a woman than bed to want to make love to her. You, on the other hand,' he added, his voice deepening, 'are different, Chloe.'

Chloe's eyebrows rose. 'Because I'm an amateur, you mean?'

'That too,' he admitted, kissing her nose. 'But until tonight I've never talked marriage to a woman before making love to her—nor at any other time.'

She gave him a narrowed, wicked smile. 'For all I know it's just the line you give any woman to entice her into bed.'

'Absolutely not. There are other ways, I assure you.'

'Don't I know it!' Chloe smiled wryly. 'I'm probably familiar with most of them. Men are ready to promise anything short of a wedding-ring in the heat of the moment.'

Piers pulled her close with sudden ferocity. 'Other men are a thing of the past, Chloe Lawrence.'

'Of course,' she said, surprised. 'All that was over long since.'

He relaxed a little, and smiled down into her eyes. 'Nevertheless, if you had so many lures thrown to you it still astonishes me that you eluded them all. You were very young. Were you never the least tempted?'

'No.' Her eyes danced. 'But then, I don't smoke either.'

'That's relevant?'

'Certainly. There's no virtue in refusing something you don't want!'

'But what about the secret lover?' he said swiftly, his eyes narrowing. 'Surely you must have wanted to make love with him?'

Her mouth set. 'You just don't understand. It's not that kind of thing, Piers. Is it so hard for you to envisage a purely cerebral longing for someone?'

'In a word, yes.' He moved his lips along her cheekbone. 'Probably because my feelings for you at this particular moment are undeniably carnal. You must know I want you again.'

She stared up at him in surprise. 'I thought at this point people either rolled over and went to sleep or smoked cigarettes.'

'Like you, I don't smoke,' he pointed out, amused. 'And only a fool would want sleep with you in his bed.'

'If that's a compliment, thank you.' She smiled at him quizzically. 'I'm not sure of the etiquette in these circumstances, but am I breaking any sexual rules if I ask to shower?'

Piers laughed, and threw back the covers, scooping her up in his arms to carry her to his bathroom. He set her on her feet, kissed her hard and ordered her to hurry.

Chloe swathed her hair in a towel and turned on the shower, lathering herself dreamily. Eyes closed, she revolved slowly, letting the water play over her body, her breath catching as she thought of Piers's caressing hands, then she gave a shriek as a tall, naked body joined her under the jet of water, and the caresses were sudden, heart-stopping reality. In breathless silence broken only by the spray of water, Piers took the soap from her and began to lather her body with long, caressing strokes. He pulled her back against him, keeping her captive with one hand at the pit of her stomach while the other traced a fiery path over her skin under the warm water flowing over them. She melted against him, knees buckling, and he turned off the spray, his hands moving up to cup her breasts, fingertips teasing nipples which rose erect to his caress, and he spun her round, flinging the towel away as he bent her backwards over his arm to take each dark, swollen bud in his mouth in turn.

Chloe clutched at him frantically and Piers tossed a pile of towels on the floor, laid her down on them and began to make love to her all over again, slowly and subtly, making up for his earlier lack of control with such artistry and skill that at the last Chloe heard her own hoarse, shaking voice pleading in the moments before she was overtaken by an overwhelming pleasure she experienced alone, her astonished eyes meeting the elation in his as he held her cruelly tight. Then she saw his eyes dilate and felt his body tense as he surrendered to the same glorious fate, and it was Chloe's turn for elation, her eyes gleaming dark as sapphires as she revelled in the power she possessed over the man in her arms.

Gwen Lawrence met her daughter at the station late the following evening, full of questions about the weekend, the party in chambers, whether Jessica had any last-minute additions to the guest list for the wedding, until eventually it dawned on her that Chloe wasn't listening to a word.

'Darling, is something the matter?' she asked anxiously.

'Mm?' said Chloe vaguely.

'I asked if there was something wrong,' said Gwen, with an emphasis which brought Chloe back to earth with a bump.

'No. Absolutely nothing,' Chloe assured her, and asked after the dogs. 'I'll take them out when we get home.'

When the dogs were back in the house and the two women were settled comfortably in the sitting-room over a tea-tray Chloe gave her parent an odd little smile as she accepted her cup.

'Mother,' she began, then halted at Gwen's look of alarm.

'What is it?' she demanded sharply. 'You never call me that.'

'Then maybe it's time I started—and there's nothing wrong, I promise you, quite the opposite.' Chloe gave her mother a luminous smile. 'Piers Audley's asked me to marry him, and I've said yes.'

Gwen Lawrence set down her teacup with an unsteady hand. 'Oh, my darling!' She held out her arms and Chloe went down on her knees and hugged her mother, swallowing on a lump in her throat.

'Are you pleased?'

Gwen returned the hug convulsively. 'I'm thrilled to bits. It's wonderful news. To be honest I'd prayed this would happen. Piers will make a quite wonderful husband, I know. And you'll make him a perfect wife, too,' she added, sniffing hard. 'I'm so very proud of you.'

Chloe sat back on her heels, frowning. 'Proud?'

Her mother blew her nose in the embroidered handkerchief she was never without, then squared her shoulders. 'I know how difficult it's been for you.'

Chloe went white. 'Difficult?'

Gwen took in a deep, unsteady breath. 'I'm not blind, darling. And I've never said a word before because I know how hard you fought against it. And I was certain you'd get over it once—once you accepted it as impossible.'

'You're telling me you've known all *along*?'

'Since you came back home to live, certainly.'

Chloe sank down on the hearthrug, shattered. 'That's a blow.' She breathed sharply, shooting a wild, stricken look at her mother. 'Does—does anyone else know?'

Her mother smiled reassuringly. 'No. Only me.'

'Actually Piers does, too.'

'What? You *told* him?'

Chloe explained how he'd chanced on her secret quite by accident the night of the party.

'And he can accept that and still want to marry you?'

'Apparently, yes. He's never been in love and considers the condition a very poor reason for marrying anyone,' said Chloe drily. 'In his book mutual liking and respect, plus a certain rapport of both mind and body, are the only necessary ingredients for a successful marriage.'

'He's not far wrong, at that.' Gwen Lawrence gave a sudden, mischievous smile. 'To be honest it was the very obvious physical rapport between you that gave me hope.'

'That he'd propose?'

'No. That he'd be the one to cure you of this obsession of yours.'

Because Piers was deeply involved in a difficult new libel action, a telephone conversation each night was Chloe's only link with him during the week.

'I can't really spare the time to travel down this weekend,' he said with an impatient sigh. 'Come to me instead.'

'I can't, Piers. It's the last weekend before Jessica's wedding. She's coming home to see to the last details.' Chloe paused. 'My mother was rather hoping you could lunch with us on Sunday in your new role as my official fiancé. She loved your letter, by the way—very graceful. So were the flowers—though you needn't have sent two lots.'

Piers chuckled. 'I can see you're going to be a provident wife. Talking of which, how long will you make me wait?'

'I was meaning to talk to you about that,' she said guardedly.

'Don't tell me you've changed your mind already!'

'Of course not.' She gave a breathless little laugh. 'It's the type of wedding I want to discuss. Would you object to something very quiet and unfussy pretty soon after Jessica's?'

'Object? It sounds like every prospective bride-groom's dream,' he said emphatically. 'The sooner and simpler the better from my point of view.' His voice deepened. 'For reasons I'm sure you'll understand.'

Chloe breathed in deeply, her colour high. 'Please come on Sunday.'

'You need me?'

'Yes, I do.'

'Then nothing will keep me away.'

The weekend was chaotic. Added to a sudden rush of last-minute wedding fever, which affected even level-headed Jessica, there was the excitement of Chloe's news.

'I couldn't believe my ears when I got home on Monday evening,' said Jess, laughing. 'Fancy leaving a message like that on my answering machine! I nearly expired with frustration trying to ring you back. I couldn't get through for ages.'

'Piers rings every night,' said Gwen happily, as she rushed about preparing a huge lunch for the family. 'Marcus, do you think this wine's suitable?'

'What for?' said Marcus, emerging from the Sunday papers. 'The food or the occasion?' He fixed Chloe with a challenging dark eye. 'Shouldn't Audley have asked *my* permission to marry you, by the way?'

'More to the point he asked mine, in a very charming letter,' said Gwen quickly. 'And sent me flowers,' she added.

'The only one he really needed to ask was Chloe,' pointed out David. 'She's a big girl now.'

Marcus eyed Chloe quizzically. 'You've turned down more than one proposal in the past to my knowledge. What's so special about this one?'

'I should have thought that was obvious,' she told him, and went off to lay the dining-room table.

By the time Piers arrived, a little after midday, Chloe'd begun to wish she'd never suggested he come to lunch in the bosom of her family. Lisa was missing, due to a cold, which meant the three doctors inevitably began to talk shop, and an acrimonious argument swiftly erupted over an article on the long-term effects of some new wonder-drug. For once Chloe let her mother play referee and escaped to her room to get ready. She changed swiftly into her suede trousers, added a heavy caramel cotton mesh sweater and brushed her hair, all the time dodging to the window every other second to watch for Piers. At last she saw his car turn into the lane and rushed downstairs to open the door just as the long green bonnet nosed down the narrow drive. As Piers jumped out she literally hurled herself into his arms.

'My darling girl, what's the matter?' he asked sharply, then kissed her before she could answer.

She smiled when he raised his head. 'I'm suffering from an excess of family. Be thankful you're an only child.'

Piers looked into her eyes searchingly. 'Is that really all?'

'I was just glad to see you.' She smiled wickedly. 'Or don't you approve of such unmaidenly enthusiasm?'

He kissed her again to show exactly how much he approved, then released her to stoop into the car for a cardboard carton. 'I thought some champagne might be a good idea, just in case your siblings disapprove of me.'

'Highly unlikely!' Chloe took his hand as they went towards the house. 'Not,' she added thoughtfully, halting on the porch, 'that it would matter if they did.'

Piers put the carton down with magnificent disregard
for its contents so he could take her in his arms and kiss
her again in appreciation.

'Are you two coming in?' said a voice from the hall,
and Chloe detached herself hastily as Jessica darted out
to greet them, David and Marcus close behind her.

'Hello, Piers,' said Jessica, beaming. She reached up
to kiss Piers's cheek. 'I'm so happy for you both.'

Piers thanked her gracefully, shook hands first with
David then with Marcus, smiling wryly at the latter. 'It's
suddenly struck me I should have written to you as well
as Mrs Lawrence.'

'As was pointed out to me earlier,' said Marcus,
shrugging, 'the only permission you really need is
Chloe's. Besides, we're all very grateful—thought we'd
never get the girl off our hands!'

Later that evening it was very quiet in the firelit sitting-
room at the Parsonage. Marcus had left an hour before,
with the intention of visiting Lisa on the way back, and
Jessica and David drove off shortly afterwards, at which
point Gwen Lawrence asked Piers if he'd think her rude
if she went to Evensong.

'Does your mother usually go to Evensong?' enquired
Piers, drawing Chloe down to the sofa.

She curled up against him with a contented little sigh.
'Sometimes. She mostly goes to early communion, but
she was too busy roasting the fatted calf this morning.'

'Very tactful of her, giving us time alone together.'

'Isn't it!' Chloe smiled up at him. 'But she won't be
long, and I imagine you won't want to be late getting
off, either.'

'No. Any other time I'd have put up at Clieve House
for the night, but I need an early start in the morning.

But first,' he added, taking a box from his pocket, 'I want you to have this.'

Chloe opened it, her eyes widening at the sight of the ring inside. She blinked as he slid it on her finger. 'Piers!' She stared at the blaze from five sapphires, each of them big enough for a respectable solitaire. She looked up into his eyes, lost for something to say.

'Don't you like it?' he asked.

'Like it! It's the most beautiful thing I've ever seen.'

He raised her hand to his lips and kissed it just above the ring. 'I was right. The stones match your eyes exactly.'

Chloe stared at her hand, mesmerised, then turned her face up to his. 'Thank you, Piers, not just for the ring, but for being here today. I needed you.'

'Not,' he said morosely, 'as much as I need you. I wish you were coming back with me tonight.'

'I wish I was, too,' she said honestly, then said no more at all for a while as Piers made love to her with a fiery tenderness that left them both tense and frustrated when he called a halt.

'I could get a special licence,' he said abruptly, and Chloe nodded, surprising him.

'Good idea.'

He breathed in deeply. 'I won't shock your mother by taking her daughter to bed while she's in church, so please don't agree with such ravishing enthusiasm, Chloe—it's bad for me.'

They lay quiet in each other's arms for a while, then Chloe stirred to look up at him.

'When are you coming down next weekend?'

'Late on Friday, too late to see you that night. What time do you want me here on Saturday morning?'

'In good time for a glass of champagne before we walk over to the church.'

Piers gazed down at her, his face inscrutable. 'Will champagne help, Chloe? I couldn't help watching you with David Warren today. Not that I—or anyone else—could have told how you feel about him, but I still wanted to hit him.'

'He doesn't deserve it, you know.' She turned her face into his shoulder, letting out a sigh. 'But I'll be glad when the wedding's over.'

His arms tightened cruelly. 'Once you're my wife,' he said forcibly, 'I'll take good care the only man you sigh over is me.'

The day of Jessica Lawrence's wedding dawned bright and blustery, but by the time Piers arrived the clouds had gone and the cool spring sun seemed willing to shine on the bride. He kissed Chloe then surveyed her with questioning eyes, but her answering smile was serene as they paused for a moment in the hall before joining the others in the drawing-room. Piers stood behind her, gazing at their reflections in the long carved mirror at the foot of the stairs, Chloe in the severe brown pin-stripes, the tall man behind her even more distinguished than usual in the sober elegance of morning dress.

'Well done,' he said quietly. 'Beautiful *and* brave.'

'Thank you.'

Their eyes met for a long moment in the mirror, then Piers dropped a sudden burning kiss where her upswept hair left the nape of neck exposed. He straightened, smiling, as Jessica came running down the stairs in a cream lace shift, her dark hair caught back with a spray of matching rosebuds. 'Hi there, Piers. Put that woman down and come and have some champagne.'

'As you can see,' said Chloe, laughing, 'the blushing bride's on top form. We only managed to chase her up to dress a few minutes ago, she's been scoffing canapés in the kitchen, and swapping rude stories with the caterers.'

'I don't see why I shouldn't enjoy my wedding-day to the full,' said Jessica, and winked. 'Not to mention the night!'

Piers's hand tightened on Chloe's as they followed the bride into the drawing-room, to join Marcus and Lisa, the latter doll-like and pretty in a silk suit and be-ribboned pillbox hat in her favourite ice blue. Gwen Lawrence, in russet wool, with a large but severely plain matching hat, came forward to welcome Piers warmly.

'How elegant you look,' she said, beaming. 'Now, just time for a glass of champagne, then we'll make our way over to the church. Jess, you and Marcus hang on until the bells stop to let the bellringers get to a pew before you arrive.'

Marcus gave Piers a wry look. 'If you'd known what you were letting yourself in for you'd probably have given our New Year's Eve thrash a wide berth.'

'On the contrary.' Piers smiled down at Chloe. 'Accepting your mother's invitation was the best move I ever made.'

She smiled up at him. 'Perhaps you'd better defer decision on that until after *our* wedding.'

'When's it to be?' said Lisa, then suddenly her eyes dropped to Chloe's hand. 'So that's your ring, Chloe.' She pulled on her white gloves with a touch of petulance. 'Very nice. A good thing you've got such long hands; mine are far too dainty for that kind of thing.'

'We hope to tie the knot as soon as possible,' answered Piers smoothly. He smiled at Gwen. 'How long do you need to get your breath back, Mrs Lawrence?'

Gwen stared from Piers to her daughter in surprise. 'I didn't dream you were in such a hurry!'

Piers smiled possessively at Chloe. 'I'm sure no one's surprised.'

Jessica laughed and gave Chloe a hug. 'A pity there's a couple of sizes difference between us, not to mention a few inches. Otherwise we could just swap dresses for the next trip to church.'

Chloe returned the hug affectionately. 'Let's concentrate on this one at the moment, bride. Where are the flowers?'

There was a sudden flurry as Marcus was despatched to fetch them from the cold old larder leading off the back entry. Chloe carefully pinned two brown-flecked cream orchids to her lapel, set a dramatic brown sombrero dead straight above her eyes, then waved Piers ahead with her mother.

'You take Gwen, Lisa and I will follow on.'

And highly incongruous we'll look, too, she thought wryly, as she gave Jessica a kiss, then looked up in astonishment as Marcus took her by the shoulders and kissed her cheek in a rare display of affection.

'You look ravishing, too,' he said and gave her a sudden little push. 'Go on, get moving.' Then, almost as an afterthought, he stooped to kiss the pouting mouth of his fiancée. 'Hurry up, Lisa. The bells will stop any moment.'

The service was moving, the bride radiant and the bridegroom handsome and only slightly nervous as he promised to love and cherish her until death did them part. A shiver ran through Chloe at the words and a long, slim hand moved to clasp hers tightly. She moved closer to Piers, almost glad of the pain as his sapphires bit into her finger under her glove.

Afterwards at the Parsonage the wedding reception was almost a repeat performance of the New Year's Eve party, except that this time Piers Audley never left

Chloe's side, receiving congratulations on their engagement in his usual self-assured way, even coaxing her to pose with him for the photographer of the local *Gazette*. He relinquished Chloe with open reluctance when it was time for her to go upstairs to help Jessica change out of her wedding-dress.

'Are you happy, love?' demanded Jessica as Chloe unzipped her.

'Shouldn't I be asking you that?' Chloe gave her a smacking kiss. 'Not that I need to. And of course I'm happy. I'm only sorry we stole some of your spotlight with our engagement. It wasn't intentional.'

'As far as I'm concerned it only added to my day,' said Jessica, and grinned. 'At least I don't have to hurl my roses at you. We know you're the next one up the aisle. By the way, something tells me Lisa wasn't too pleased about that. Stealing her thunder a bit.'

Chloe made a face, then cast an eye round the chaos in the room. 'I think I'd better square things up here to make sure you haven't forgotten anything. If you're ready go on down, I'll bring your overnight case when I've finished.'

Chloe moved quickly about the room, tidying Jessica's belongings into drawers, checking that her sister's passport was in the zipper compartment of her overnight bag. She added a paperback novel she'd bought Jessica for the flight then put the suitcase near the door and turned back to the dressing table to tidy her hair. She looked up as she saw the door open, then stiffened as she saw the tall, handsome man reflected in the mirror. He shut the door behind him and stood against it and she turned casually.

'You've come in for Jess's case?'

'Officially, yes.' His face wore a disquieting expression she'd never seen before. 'But that was just an excuse. We're off soon and I needed a moment alone with you.'

'Why?'

'Before I go, tell me why you're in such a hell of a hurry to marry Audley,' he said grimly. 'Is there a reason?'

Chloe's chin lifted. 'If you mean am I pregnant, no. Or not,' she added with a secret little smile, 'as far as I know.'

He moved towards her, jaw clenched. 'You're sleeping with him?'

She thrust out her left hand with its blaze of sapphires. 'It's not unknown in the circumstances.'

'But the first time for you, isn't it? *Isn't it*?' he added through his teeth.

She stared. 'How can you possibly know that?'

He smiled scornfully. 'The only real relationship you ever had was with Mick Streeter, and Mick's not interested in women that way, is he? Anyway,' he added, moving closer, 'if I didn't know before I know now. You look—different. Sleeping Beauty's awake at last.'

'You're angry,' she said slowly, frowning. 'Why?'

He gave a mirthless laugh. 'Because I'm so bloody jealous I could do murder. Audley's stolen what should rightfully be mine, and you know it. I just didn't wake up to the fact until I saw you two together last week.' His jaw clenched. 'I had a job to keep from punching him—he couldn't keep his hands off you.'

Chloe's eyes widened in deep dismay, alarm bells clamouring in her head as he reached for her. She backed away hastily, but caught her heel in the bedside rug, and with a triumphant laugh he snatched her in his arms, almost cracking her ribs as he bent his head for the kiss she'd always dreamed of. Only this was more nightmare than dream. There was desperation and anger instead of tenderness in the mouth which forced hers apart. He was crushing the life out of her and, tragically, all she felt in response was shame and embarrassment. Then suddenly she lost her temper, and began to fight like a wildcat, but she was no match for his strength or his temper as he ground his mouth into hers, one large hand grasping a handful of her hair to hold her still.

Suddenly his arms slackened and Chloe spun round, ready to run, then froze, the blood draining from her face as she saw Piers in the doorway, his tawny eyes blazing with disgust and revulsion as he took in the tableau before him.

'Dear God in heaven,' he said bitterly, as if someone had just punched him in the stomach. 'So that was it all along! What a stupid bloody fool I've been.' His face set like a mask. 'Incest never crossed my mind.'

Marcus brushed past Chloe to put a hand on his arm. 'You don't understand——'

Piers shook him off in violent distaste. 'Get your hands off me, you bastard! You two had better pull yourselves together and get downstairs. The bride and groom are ready to leave.'

CHAPTER TEN

CHLOE'S skill as an actress had never stood her in better stead. Desperate to be alone with Piers to explain, she somehow managed to keep her smile in place as the happy pair drove off to cries of good wishes and the clanking of cans tied to the bumper of David's car. The moment the rear light disappeared up the drive the usual feeling of anticlimax filled the air and guests began to leave. But Piers remained obdurately in the background, his face averted as he chatted to David's parents while Chloe was obliged to stand with her mother and Marcus to see everyone off, her brain reeling with the shock of the episode in Jessica's bedroom.

Her heart leapt as Piers finally came to join them, but it was to her mother he spoke.

'Mrs Lawrence, would you excuse me? Now I can get at my car I'd like to dash back to Clieve House to change.'

'Of course, my dear,' said Gwen. 'Take Chloe with you, if you like.'

He shook his head, ignoring the entreaty in Chloe's eyes. 'I'll only be a few minutes. It's like a building site up there—no place to linger.'

'Piers——' began Chloe, putting out a hand, but he moved out of reach.

'It won't take long.' He strode from the house quickly, and she stared after him in despair for a moment, then pinned the smile back on her face and went off to the kitchen to organise some tea for those remaining behind.

A moment later Marcus came in, slamming the door behind him, his face grim as he saw the desolation in Chloe's eyes.

'Don't look like that!' he said swiftly, starting towards her, then halted at her recoil. 'No need for that, I won't make the same mistake twice. And when Audley comes back I'll explain to him,' he added, reddening. 'Anyway, I thought he knew you weren't my real sister. I'm hellish sorry, Chlo—I never meant all that to happen.'

'What use is that now?' she said tightly, putting cups and saucers on a tray. She gave him a long, perplexed look, wondering why he was suddenly different. All her adult life he'd been all she ever wanted. Now, in the space of a few minutes, all that was changed. Only it was nothing to do with Marcus. It was she who'd undergone the change, and not in a few minutes at all, but from the moment she'd first set eyes on Piers Audley.

'Will you stop looking at me like that!' he said bitterly. 'I'm no monster.'

'You behaved like one upstairs.' Chloe raised a hostile eyebrow. 'Isn't it time you got back to Lisa, Marcus?'

Marcus looked sick. He threw out his hands in entreaty. 'She mustn't know about this.'

Chloe poured boiling water into a teapot, her mouth set. 'It's not something to exchange girlish confidences about, is it! Nor will Piers discuss it either, you can be sure of that. Here. Take this tray to the drawing-room, please.'

Marcus hefted the tray and hesitated, a strange, dull look in his eyes. 'Chloe, I suppose there's no chance——?'

'None!' she retorted bluntly, and his jaw set.

'Do you love him?' he asked, as though the words burnt like acid on his tongue.

Her eyes clouded over with despair. 'Oh, yes, Marcus, I love him. Quite desperately. Unfortunately I only discovered that just now, up in Jess's bedroom. I suppose I should be grateful to you for waking me up to the fact. Not that it matters. Something tells me Piers wouldn't touch me with a bargepole now, however much you try to explain.'

Chloe's gut feeling was right. Piers rang soon afterwards, to tell her she was at liberty to manufacture what fiction she liked, but to make his apologies to her mother for his absence. 'I'm driving straight back to town right now.'

'Piers—please! Let me *explain*,' she whispered urgently, afraid someone would overhear.

'Don't be stupid!' he said with cold violence. 'What I saw was self-explanatory.' And he rang off before she could say another word.

Chloe kept up a remarkably good front until quite late that night, when the Parsonage was quiet and she was alone with her mother.

'So why didn't Piers come back this evening? I wouldn't have thought barristers got called away like doctors and engineers,' said Gwen.

Chloe explained as unemotionally as she could.

Her mother heard her out in stricken silence then hugged her close. 'Go and ring him up at once.'

'I already have, but he wasn't there. I left a message on his answering machine, asking him to ring back. But he won't,' said Chloe brokenly. 'And after what he believes he saw, you can't really blame him.'

'If you like I'll leave a message and ask him to talk to *me*,' offered Gwen. 'I can put matters right in a couple of seconds if he'll just listen. Which,' she added thoughtfully, 'he's far more likely to do in my case, if only out of sheer good manners.'

'No, thanks, Mother.' Chloe lifted the hair from her neck wearily. 'I don't think there's any possible chance of mending things between us, but if there is it's down to me to make it happen.'

As Chloe forecast, there was no telephone call that night, nor the next day, despite the two urgent messages she left. Piers, it was obvious, couldn't stomach the thought of talking to her, even down a telephone line. Chloe got through her working day on the Monday like an automaton, part of her coping with her job with her usual efficiency, the rest of her screaming with pain inside. She drove home like a maniac that evening, certain there would be a message from Piers, but one look at her mother's face killed any hope.

'Nothing?' she said dully.

'No, darling. Ring him again.'

But the sound of Piers's drawl on his answering machine yet again was so shattering that this time Chloe couldn't even bring herself to leave a message.

When the telephone did ring later that night Chloe flew to answer it in breathless hope, but it was Marcus, to ask whether she'd managed to patch things up with Piers. When she enlightened him he swore volubly and demanded Piers's address so he could go round and set him straight.

'No way,' she said emphatically. 'The last person he wants to see is you at this moment in time. But thanks for the offer.'

Chloe went back to the sitting-room to tell her mother it hadn't been Piers, not that it was necessary to explain. Her drawn, unhappy face said it all for her. 'Strange, really,' added Chloe wearily. 'Marcus obviously never had the slightest idea how I felt. While I've wasted half my life mooning over some ideal I'd built up in my mind about him. I realise now that all began to change the moment I met Piers. I was drawn to him from the first, but now it's too late. I feel so—so angry with myself.'

'Thank heaven Marcus never did know how you felt, Chloe,' said Gwen soberly. 'Marcus may be a dedicated doctor, but where his own desires are concerned he can sometimes be just as single-minded. Piers could have walked in on something far more serious if Marcus had suspected——'

'I had a stupid, immature crush on him?'

Gwen nodded. 'I think Marcus never quite managed to look on you as a sister once the carrot-topped ugly duckling turned into a swan so suddenly. Why was he so furious about the modelling, and so ready, always, to thump anyone who looked sideways at you? Fortunately the penny never really dropped for him until you decided to marry Piers.'

Chloe eyed her mother curiously. 'Why fortunately? Marcus and I are not actually related in any way.'

'No, but as you've just learnt so cruelly, you'd have been utterly wrong for each other. I've always known that. And I was so afraid Marcus might suddenly wake up to his own feelings one day that it was like sitting on a time-bomb sometimes!'

When several days passed with no word from Piers Chloe faced facts. There wasn't going to be any word from him. To make matters worse the local weekly news-paper, the *Gazette*, carried not one, but two photographs of the Lawrence/Warren wedding, one of the bride and groom and one of Chloe with Piers Audley, with a caption proclaiming her engagement to the well-known barrister.

Chloe's heart contracted as she stared at the smiling faces in the photograph. She pushed the paper away and sat, dry-eyed, gazing into space.

'Why not ring his chambers?' suggested Gwen, but Chloe shook her head firmly.

'He'd just refuse to speak to me, and I couldn't bear that.' She smiled bleakly. 'I think it's time I took the hint, don't you? I'll just send the ring back with a brief explanation and retire from the lists. He doesn't want me any more.'

With a heavy heart Chloe packaged the ring, and sent it with a letter to Piers at his chambers, explaining briefly that the Reverend George Lawrence had married Gwen, the widow of the previous vicar at Little Compton, when Chloe was less than a year old. He'd adopted the baby as his own, to be brought up as a Lawrence like his own children, Marcus and Jessica. 'You were wrong about the incest,' she wrote in conclusion, 'my sin was of omission. I merely let you draw the wrong conclusion.'

His response was prompt, brief, and quite lethal to any last lingering hope she'd cherished. The letter was signed by the typist instructed by Mr Audley to inform Miss Lawrence, with his thanks, that he was in safe receipt of the registered package.

In the days that followed Chloe had cause to be grateful for her busy, demanding job. Propax Pharmaceuticals had taken her on only months after she'd completed her business course, and in the beginning life as a secretary after the frenetic rush of her modelling career had taken some adjustment. But once her colleagues got used to the idea that someone as decorative as Chloe Lawrence could also be efficient, good at her job and totally conscientious, they accepted her without question.

After the punishing hours and hectic lifestyle of her modelling days Chloe found the regular nine-to-five routine very much to her taste. Both her innate skill with the written word and the newly learned skill with the indispensable technology employed in the company's offices, soon had her climbing the promotion ladder to her present post as personal assistant to the marketing director. An astute, successful businessman, he quickly recognised the high degree of competence which lay behind his new assistant's misleading exterior and worked Chloe almost as hard as himself. And she was never more grateful for it than now, not caring how much work he heaped on her if it helped fill at least some of the aching void left by Piers.

When the newly-weds returned from their three-week honeymoon Jess was appalled to find Chloe unattached again.

'It didn't work out,' said Chloe flatly, and refused to elaborate to a Jessica quietened only by a very speaking look from Gwen Lawrence.

At the end of a particularly tiring week Chloe went for her regular walk with the dogs when she got home. Her mother was playing bridge at the Dawsons, consequently Chloe stayed out longer than usual, hoping to tire herself out enough to sleep for once, and it was almost dark when she turned through the Parsonage gates. She let the dogs off the leads and as usual they tore down the long drive and round to the back of the house and the bowls of water kept in the back entry. Chloe followed on, yawning, then paused, frowning, sure she could hear something behind her. Suddenly the world exploded in pain and she dropped like a stone into the arms waiting for her.

When Chloe came to she was trussed and gagged and bumping about in the close confines of the boot of a car. Her head hurt abominably and though she felt sick and panic-stricken, her worst problem by far was claustrophobia. She forced herself to breathe evenly, to ignore the fact that she was shut in such a small space, and tried not to think what might happen if she threw up while she lay gagged and helpless. As she fought her rebellious stomach she realised the car was slowing down. She brightened. She wasn't being taken far. Unless she'd been unconscious for hours, in which case she could be miles and miles from home for all she knew. Then suddenly the car began bumping madly over what felt like a rutted, unmade track, throwing her all over the place before the vehicle came to a stop.

The boot opened up and hands reached in to drag her out. She was tossed over someone's shoulder and gave a choking groan, the pain in her head excruciating as the blood rushed to the place where she'd been struck. She was barely conscious by the time she was dumped down and the gag removed.

'If you scream I'll shove it back in,' said a muffled male voice, but Chloe, quite incapable of speech by this time, made no sound other than a gasp of fear as her companion shone a torch in her eyes. 'Tut, tut,' sneered the voice. 'Top model Chloe Lawrence looks like something the cat dragged in. Pity that bastard Audley can't see you now. Or perhaps it's all to the good. He wouldn't want you back in that state, would he?'

'Who are you?' demanded Chloe hoarsely. 'Where is this? Why have——?' She stopped dead as the gag appeared in front of her eyes.

'No questions!' threatened the man, with such menace she subsided, trembling. 'Right. I'm going to leave you alone here tonight. Don't worry. No one will bother you here, in case you're wondering. There's a bucket in the corner and a blanket on the camp bed. And out of the kindness of my heart I'm going to untie your hands and feet.' He let out the same muffled, chilling laugh as he untied her. 'But don't get too optimistic, lady. Once I've locked the door you haven't a hope in hell of getting out. Sweet dreams.'

Chloe was so furiously angry that she would have gone for his eyes with her nails if her hands and feet hadn't been useless. Her bonds had been so tight the pain was intense as the blood rushed back and by the time her limbs were in working order again her gaoler was long gone. Her watch, she found, had broken at some stage, so she had no idea of the time. She'd been dumped on a rickety camp bed designed for someone less long in the leg, and the blanket her exploring hands found was smelly and thin. Thankful she'd changed into sweater and jeans and her old sheepskin jacket before taking the dogs out, she sat very still for a while, husbanding her strength.

Her head hurt abominably, but as her nausea gradually subsided her rumbling stomach reminded her that coffee and a sandwich had been her only food that day. Gingerly her fingers explored the bump on her head and came away sticky. Hoping her tetanus injections were up to date, she wished vainly that she had a light, then set out to use hands instead of eyes to explore her prison. Feeling her way round the walls, Chloe found she was in a small room with a sloping ceiling, obviously an attic. There were two windows low down in the wall, each of them tiny and half-moon shaped, cobwebby to the touch and located only by two slightly less dense slivers of darkness in their vicinity. The only furniture was the bed, and the plastic bucket she discovered by kicking it over. Making a face, she tried to ignore that particular problem, and made her way back to the bed. If she were sensible, Chloe told herself firmly, she'd lie down and try to sleep. Only it was desperately hard to be sensible in her present situation. For one thing she felt thirsty, and her head hurt badly, but not badly enough to take her mind off her hunger. And she was very, very cold.

Chloe curled up on the bed, wrapping the malodorous blanket round her, thinking hard about her kidnapper. He obviously knew Piers in some way. Did the maniac think he could demand some kind of ransom for her? If so, he was in for a nasty shock. Piers didn't want her back. Chloe's teeth chattered suddenly. If the man realised she was of no value to him he might just kill her. And suddenly Chloe realised just how much she wanted to live, Piers or no Piers. Things would look better in daylight, she assured herself. And once she could see where she was she might be able to escape.

Head throbbing, racked by thoughts of the anguish her mother must be experiencing, Chloe spent a miserable, sleepless night, glad when dawn came at last. But as the light increased she learned very little more than she knew already. The door had been reinforced with boards and a new, formidable lock, and the windows were very small. Added to which there was no way of telling how far the drop might be to what appeared to be a deserted farmyard below.

When she heard a car Chloe tensed, then did her best to tidy herself. She sat erect, her eyes glittering in her ashen face, as heavy footsteps thumped on the stairs, then a key turned in the lock and her gaoler came in and slammed the door behind him. He was no taller than herself, clad in denims and a heavy sweater, both garments surprisingly clean and new, like the woollen balaclava which covered his head and face except for holes for eyes and mouth. He dumped a carrier bag down on the floor and advanced towards her, brandishing a small tape recorder.

'Right then, Chloe. Had a good night?' He laughed at her violent recoil. 'Don't worry, sweetheart. You're safe from me! I like my women dark, with nice round hips, and breasts I can get my hands on. And clean!' he added, enjoying her resentful glare.

Annoyed with herself for letting her feelings show, Chloe sat without moving a muscle as he squatted down in front of her.

'Now then. You shall have a nice cup of tea from a thermos and a sandwich if you say your little piece in here.'

Chloe stared at him stonily. 'And if I don't?'

He scratched his head through the balaclava, pretending to think. 'Which would you prefer, eh? Another bump on the head, or a go at changing my mind?'

'About letting me go?' she asked swiftly, then clenched her fists as he threw back his masked head and roared with laughter.

'That's a good one,' he gasped at last, and leaned forward confidentially. 'I meant about the brunettes. I've never had a skinny redhead, but you never know—nearer the bone, sweeter the meat, they say.'

Chloe stared at her gaoler with bored eyes, hoping he couldn't tell she was panicking inside. 'That's no choice at all. I'll take the bump on the head.'

For a moment she was convinced he'd take her at her word, then the man shook his head. 'You're a cool one, I'll give you that.'

Cool! thought Chloe.

'Go on,' he urged, holding out the tape recorder. 'Talk to Audley on that. I can just picture the jerk squirming!'

'I doubt that he will,' said Chloe with polite regret. 'Mr Audley and I are no longer engaged.'

'You're lying!' he snarled. 'I saw it in the paper.' He thrust his face towards her until she could smell his breath as he spoke. 'I want the bastard to know I've got his woman at my mercy, to do what I like with, so talk into the bloody machine right now or I'll send one of your fingers to Audley instead.'

Chloe could have borne a knock on the head. Having her finger chopped off was something else entirely. Coward! she raged at herself, feeling sick. She raised her chin with hauteur.

'Very well. What do you want me to say?'

Ten minutes later she was alone, with a thermos of tea and a packet of sandwiches for company, and a long, long time stretching in front of her to reflect on the perils of her situation.

She drank some of the tea thirstily, mulling over the information her kidnapper had given her before he locked her in again. As she'd expected, he was after the usual extortionate ransom money. But his main motive was revenge. What he wanted most of all was the satisfaction of Piers Audley frantic at the thought of Chloe in the hands of a man he'd once sent to gaol.

'You mean Piers Audley prosecuted you?' she'd asked.

'No bloody fear. He was defending me! Best defence counsel in the business, they said, but he didn't get *me* off.'

'Were you innocent?'

The man chuckled. 'Don't be daft!'

'Then why the revenge?'

'Because, you stupid cow, if he'd got me off I'd still have Bonnie.'

'Bonnie?'

He nodded his masked head. 'What a body!' He made a gesture in the air with his hands. 'Like a centrefold from a girlie magazine. But Bonnie had very expensive tastes. I was just a clerk in an electronics company and I needed money to keep her happy so I doctored some accounts. Only I got caught.' His fists clenched. 'Bonnie swore blind she'd wait for me, but the slag never even bothered to visit. Next thing I hear she's shacked up with a crook who runs a string of amusement arcades.'

Chloe restricted herself to one cheese sandwich and a small quantity of tea, knowing it was only sensible to save some of her provisions for later since her gaoler had informed her, with false regret, that he couldn't get back until next day. She shivered at the prospect of another cold, lonely night, and wondered how Piers would feel when he got her recorded message. She'd tried hard to sound brave, but her voice had wavered uncontrollably towards the end, which had given her gaoler much satisfaction. He'd assured her he was driving to London to get the message delivered by courier to Piers Audley this very day.

Chloe had her doubts about Piers's readiness to pay ransom for a woman he no longer wanted, but she felt a little better after the food. No knight on a charger was coming to her rescue, that was certain, so somehow or other she had to try to get herself out of here. She got down on her hands and knees in front of the nearest semi-circle of filthy glass to look out. Now the light was better she could see that the farmhouse was not only deserted, but derelict. By crawling from one window to the other she gained a general impression of barns and cowsheds down below, but there were holes in the roofs, and the walls were in ruins in places. Which meant that no one ever came here. She thought for a moment then slid off her jacket and wrapped the heavy sheepskin round her hand and arm so she could take a punch at the window to break the glass. Her first attempt was

unsuccessful, resulting in an ungainly sprawl of arms
and legs on the floor, and more throbbing in her head.

Ignoring it, Chloe distributed her weight more carefully and took another swipe at the glass with her heavily
swathed fist, successful this time as one of the small
panes broke, and a shower of broken glass rained down
outside. In a sudden burst of furious energy she punched
at the remaining panes again and again, switching to her
left hand when her right hand grew painful, until all the
glass was gone and part of the frame with it. Chloe's
eyes lit up as she worked with a will to dislodge the rest
of the frame, succeeding partly through her own efforts
but mostly because the wood was rotten after years of
neglect, except for one section which refused to budge
from one side. When she'd finished the aperture was
still small, but now, she found, sobbing for breath, she
could at least lean out to look for any possibility of an
escape route.

Chloe was unsurprised to find the distance to the
ground too much to risk simply letting herself drop from
the window, even if she could manage to wriggle her
entire body through it. She took a moment or two to
get her breath back then saw that away to her left a
drainpipe wreathed in ivy descended from the ancient
guttering along the eaves to the ground below. Chloe
eyed it with sudden excitement. If she could manage to
wriggle out and stretch far enough she might just reach
it. You *must* reach it, she told herself flatly, and withdrew
her head. She took a breather, deciding that maybe this
was the time to eat another sandwich to boost her energy
for what was likely to be a very tricky climb. Even if
she were lucky enough to reach the drainpipe there was
no guarantee it would withstand her weight.

Knowing she'd need it if she got down, Chloe flung
her jacket down to the yard below, then took in a deep

breath, let it out again slowly and began to wriggle her way through the aperture. With all the skill of a limbo dancer, she managed to manoeuvre herself somewhat painfully through the opening until she was sitting on the bare bricks of the window sill, clinging to the upper arch with both hands and her back to the ground below. She sat still for a moment, then looked sideways at the ivy-covered pipe. If she inched her way to the farthest side of the aperture and held on to the sliver of wood left on the brickwork she might just be able to lean far enough to grasp the pipe, or at least the ivy, with her right.

For the first time in her life Chloe blessed her height and reach. She closed her eyes for a second, said a little prayer, then leaned sideways as far as she could, hand and arm outstretched, and to her horror almost over-balanced. She grabbed wildly to her right, her fingers scrabbling for purchase on the ivy before they managed to close on the bracket which held the pipe to the wall. Convinced she'd fall any minute, she let the one hand take her weight very slowly as she freed her legs little by little and hung at last by both hands from the creaking, protesting drainpipe. Then her seeking foot found a toe-hold on the ivy and she began to inch her way down with agonising slowness. She was within feet of the ground when the inevitable finally happened. The pipe came away from the wall with a great rending sound, taking ivy and Chloe with it to crash down together on to the earth below.

Chloe lay sprawled for some time, sobbing for breath, aching all over, but euphoric to find herself alive. And not only alive but with nothing broken as far as she could tell when she moved her arms and legs experimentally. The pipe had missed her by inches, she found, when she staggered to her feet to stare down at it. And she was bruised and filthy, her hands were swollen and sore, her head thumped and her ankle protested, but none of it mattered because she'd managed, against all odds, to escape. She retrieved her jacket, glad of its warmth against a sudden attack of shivers, then hobbled away hurriedly, determined to get as far from the derelict farm as possible before her kidnapper came back to find the bird had flown.

The farm was in the middle of woodland, with only a deserted, rutted track to give Chloe any idea of where to go. It led her to a narrow, pot-holed road where no traffic of any kind passed her for what seemed like miles, but she forced herself on, teeth clenched. Her ankle was threatening to give out altogether before she noticed smoke, then to her enormous relief a pair of cottages came into view round a bend in the road.

There was no reply when she knocked on the first door, but she had better luck with the second house. A pleasant-faced woman opened the top half of a stable-type door to the sound of furious barking. She looked at Chloe enquiringly, then with sudden alarm as she took in her disreputable appearance.

'Good evening. Would you be kind enough to let me use your phone?' said Chloe politely, and tried to smile. 'My name's Chloe Lawrence, and I've had rather an unpleasant experience. I'm anxious to let my mother know I'm all right.'

CHAPTER ELEVEN

CHLOE'S choice of request was inspired. Mention of her mother changed the woman's attitude completely. She drew Chloe inside the cottage, pushing away an excited sheepdog as she listened to a brief, edited version of the kidnap, exclaiming in horror at every other word. She introduced herself as Mrs Iris Taylor, delighted Chloe by telling her this was Ploughton, a village barely twenty miles from Little Compton, and showed her filthy guest to a bathroom. Promising hot tea as soon as she got back from next door to ask to use the phone, she apologised for lack of one herself.

'You're very kind,' said Chloe gratefully. 'I must have frightened you to death, turning up on your doorstep in this state.'

'I won't say you didn't,' said the woman frankly. 'I was ready to bang the door in your face until you spoke, that's a fact.'

When Chloe emerged from the small, spotless bathroom, feeling very much better, her hostess was hovering outside in distress.

'They're not in next door, they go out sometimes on Saturdays.'

'Is there a phone box nearby?'

'Couple of miles down the road.' Mrs Taylor wrung her hands. 'It's my husband's night out tonight, too. Darts match. Tell you what,' she added suddenly, 'you drink some tea and have something to eat, then I'll drive you home. My Brian's got a lift tonight, so his truck's outside.'

The pick-up was old, but Mrs Taylor proved to be a competent, steady driver, well able to cope with its idiosyncrasies. Chloe had meant to ask to stop at the phone box, but fell asleep almost at once, and only woke up when Mrs Taylor needed instructions to find the Parsonage as they neared Little Compton.

As the pick-up nosed down the drive Chloe's heart gave a great leap in her chest as she saw Piers's car parked alongside David's, and the smart new roadster Lisa had been given by her parents for her birthday. 'I'm afraid there's quite a reception committee,' she said unsteadily.

'Only natural seeing you'd gone missing,' said Mrs Taylor, and smiled rather shyly. 'Lovely old place you live in. But now you're safe and sound I'll be off back home.'

'Certainly not,' said Chloe indignantly. 'You must come in and meet my family and have something to eat and drink at the very least. My mother would never forgive me if I let you go off without a word!'

'I don't know about that, dear.' Mrs Taylor cast a doubtful look at her neat jumper and skirt. 'I'm not dressed——'

Chloe let out a gurgle of laughter. 'Compared with me you're a vision of elegance, Mrs Taylor. Besides——' she winced as she tried her foot '—I'm afraid I'll have to ask you to knock at the door. I don't think I can get down from here on this ankle. It's a bit swollen.'

At once Mrs Taylor was all concern. She jumped down from the truck, eager to alert Chloe's family that a doctor was needed at once.

Chloe, light-headed from a variety of emotions, gave a rather hysterical chuckle, assuring her that one knock on the door was all it would take to bring not one, but probably three doctors rushing to her aid.

But when the Parsonage door opened to Mrs Taylor it was Piers who shot from the house first, like a sprinter from the starting blocks. The three doctors came in hot pursuit just behind as he raced to the pick-up, Gwen Lawrence and Lisa bringing up the rear, with the two retrievers rushing about and barking to add to the chaos, and everyone talking at once.

'Darling, are you all right?' demanded Piers hoarsely through the hubbub, and without waiting for her answer gathered her up in his arms and held her close for several moments before he carried her into the house, with the others close behind, Gwen pulling Mrs Taylor by the hand after her as Chloe asked to be taken to the kitchen.

'I'm too dirty to put anywhere else,' she said breathlessly. Piers set her down on a chair as though she were made of spun glass, his eyes murderous as he took in the state of her, and at once the babble broke out again as everyone asked questions simultaneously, with Mrs Taylor looking rather overcome, until Gwen recollected herself and asked her to sit down, holding up a hand for silence.

'First of all,' she said, hugging Chloe close, 'are you—hurt in any way?'

Chloe returned the hug convulsively, burying her face on her mother's shoulder. 'A knock on the head, some cuts and bruises and my ankle hurts, but otherwise I'm fine.' She sat back in the chair to look up at Piers. 'I didn't expect to find *you* here.'

His mouth twisted. His eyes were bloodshot, with dark marks under them, and except for his clothes he looked in hardly better shape than Chloe. 'I had a phone call last night from the man who abducted you, then a tape with your voice on it today. I've only just got here myself.'

Gwen shuddered. 'When I got home last night to find the dogs roaming loose and you nowhere in sight I was frantic. Then Piers rang shortly afterwards to say you'd been kidnapped!'

Marcus swore violently, and dropped down in front of Chloe, taking her wrist in his hand to feel her pulse. 'Tell me the truth. Did the bastard molest you in any way, Chloe?'

Heat rose in her cheeks. 'No, he didn't!' she said irritably, embarrassed. She smiled crookedly at Piers. 'The man's taste didn't run to skinny redheads. He's pining for a voluptuous brunette by the name of Bonnie—and blames you for her loss.'

Jessica exclaimed in surprise. 'Good heavens—why?'

Piers looked blank. 'I haven't the faintest idea. I didn't know the voice, which was muffled purposely, probably. And I'm definitely not acquainted with any lady called Bonnie, brunette or otherwise.'

Chloe smiled a little. 'I'll explain later.' She cast a grateful look at Mrs Taylor, who appeared slightly dazed by all the excitement. 'When I escaped I was lucky enough to knock on Mrs Taylor's door for help. She doesn't have a phone so she very kindly drove me home. Isn't it time someone gave her a drink?'

At once Mrs Taylor was inundated with offers of food, alcohol, tea, coffee, and a more comfortable location suggested as somewhere to enjoy whichever choice she made. When a nice cup of coffee met with her approval, Jess flew to make it while Chloe gave a short, expurgated version of her adventure to the assembled company, after which Gwen asked Piers to carry her daughter upstairs so Chloe could have a bath and get to bed, where Jessica could see to her ankle and all her other hurts.

Chloe, who by this time was feeling decidedly less than her best, gave in without a struggle, except to ask Mrs Taylor for her address. 'When I feel more human—and look it—I'll come and see you again.' She smiled. 'Only you'll have to give me directions. I slept all the way home, to my shame, so I still don't have a clue where your house actually is.'

Piers carried Chloe carefully upstairs in silence, only the thump of his heart against her cheek giving her any clue as to his emotions. Jessica, following behind, instructed him to deposit his burden in the bathroom, then looked at Piers militantly.

'When she's clean and I've done my ministering angel bit you can come back up and see her. You've probably got a lot to say to her.'

Piers smiled bleakly. 'The understatement of the year. Perhaps you should ask Chloe whether she wants me to say it.'

'Oh, don't talk rubbish,' said Jess forcefully, and waved him away. 'You look terrible. You need a brandy or something.'

'I need something,' he agreed, looking at Chloe. 'But it's not brandy.'

'Dear me,' said Jessica, as the bathroom door closed behind him. 'Can it be that our legal eagle was worried about you?' She turned on the taps then began to help Chloe off with her clothes. 'Dear heaven, Chlo, what have you done to your hands?'

'I had to break a window.' Chloe let herself gingerly into the bath, every part of her stinging or throbbing as her various hurts came in contact with the hot water Jess laced liberally with antiseptic.

'Shall I wash your hair?' asked Jess thickly, blinking back a very unprofessional tear at the sight of her sister's bruises.

'Yes, please, only careful with the bump at the back. The man mugged me before giving me a joyride in his boot.'

Jess stared in horror. 'In his boot! Oh, love, how did you cope with your claustrophobia?'

Chloe pulled a face. 'Badly. As a travelling companion it's the pits! Now help me get clean quickly, please—only for mercy's sake be gentle, Doctor.'

After a bath, a shampoo, a tetanus injection and some expert strapping on her ankle, Chloe pulled on a striped green nightshirt and climbed into bed to subside with a sigh against the pillows Jess piled behind her.

'I'll go down and let Gwen come up, if she's finished smothering Mrs Taylor with gratitude,' said Jessica, eyeing her handiwork. 'Hm. You look a lot better than when you arrived.'

'I'd have a job to look worse!'

They laughed unsteadily together, then Jess went running down the stairs, and a moment later Gwen came in to embrace her child and make sure all was well with her before she let Piers come up.

'Thank God you're safe, darling,' she said at last, when she could bear to tear herself away.

'Amen to that,' agreed Chloe soberly. She took in a deep breath. 'I hope things haven't been awkward for you. With Marcus and Piers together, I mean.'

Gwen shook her head, her eyes twinkling. 'Once Piers found Lisa was here with Marcus he thawed towards him, strangely enough. But worry over you was the real leveller. All everyone could think of was getting you back again in one piece.'

When Piers came in a few minutes later Chloe looked at him in silence.

'How are you feeling?' he asked.

'Better.' She smiled politely. 'Just to be clean again is quite wonderful.'

Piers pulled a chair near the bed and sat down, eyeing her with rather less than his usual smooth assurance. 'I'm bloody sorry you've been subjected to such an ordeal, Chloe.'

'It wasn't your fault.'

'Of course it was my fault! The man only abducted you to injure *me*, remember.' He breathed in deeply. 'It was bad enough getting the telephone message last night——'

'But lucky,' she put in.

He frowned. 'Lucky?'

'That you answered the man. All I ever got was your machine,' she said coolly.

He winced. 'You haven't tried lately, Chloe.'

'No. I gave up the day I sent the ring back—no, I tell a lie,' she added musingly. 'I really gave up the day I got the letter saying you'd received it.'

'Let's leave that for the moment,' he said grimly. 'First I want to know who abducted you. When I heard the tape I went berserk. The quaver in your voice cut me to pieces.'

'It wasn't intentional,' she assured him wearily, 'but it pleased my gaoler quite a bit.'

'What was he like? Describe him to me.'

'I can't help much. He wore a woollen balaclava over his head the whole time, regulation terrorist type, so I never saw his face. He's a bit taller than me, but burly— and strong, because he carried me over his shoulder up the stairs to the attic where I was kept.'

'Mrs Taylor believes the place you were held is called Fleck's Farm, by the way,' he put in. 'Disused for years, apparently, with a reputation for being haunted.'

'Perfect!' Chloe shivered. 'I'm glad I didn't know *that* last night.'

'I've told the police. They'll be ready and waiting for the bastard when he gets back there.' He paused, his eyes locked with hers. 'Did he stay with you?'

'No, thankfully. He just dumped me, locked me in and took off.' She tried to smile. 'I'd been walking the dogs so I was wearing my sheepskin jacket, otherwise I'd have been frozen. The blanket he provided wasn't much comfort.'

Piers leaned closer, his face intent. 'Tell me all you can about the man, Chloe. Think hard.'

'I don't need to. When he came back today he told me he wanted to get back at you because you'd failed to get him off on an embezzlement charge. He was a clerk in an electronics firm, if that means anything to you. He fiddled with the books to get money to lavish on the beautiful Bonnie. Because he got sent down, and Bonnie immediately transferred her attentions to a richer bird in the hand, he feels you ruined his life. Making off with me as revenge was obviously more important to him than any ransom money.'

Piers nodded slowly in comprehension. 'Ronald William Hicks, as I live and breathe.' He shook his head. 'I wouldn't have thought he had it in him—he seemed a pretty mild, inoffensive type.'

'Not any more.' Chloe pulled a face. 'His time in prison must have changed him. Not only did he give me a crack on the head, he threatened to chop off one of my fingers as a gift for you if I didn't record the message.'

Piers went white and reached for her hand, then breathed in sharply as he saw the swollen knuckles and the rope-marks round her wrist. 'You must be cursing the day you ever laid eyes on me,' he said bitterly. 'I could murder the swine for hurting you.'

Chloe withdrew the hand firmly. 'That kind of hurt I can cope with. The kind you dished out was far harder to bear.'

Piers winced, and got up restlessly, going over to the window to gaze down into the dark garden. 'I can be forgiven for some of my reaction, Chloe. Surely you can imagine how I felt when I found you in the arms of your brother!'

'Of course I can. I can even understand the refusal to answer my phone calls,' she said hotly. 'But to send a message via a typist after I explained was utterly brutal.'

'I don't see why.' Piers swung round to look at her. 'It was a relief to know you weren't related to Marcus, I'll admit. But it didn't make things much better otherwise from my point of view.'

Chloe stared at him blankly. 'I don't understand.'

He came back to the bed and stood over her. 'Think. I found you in the arms of the man you'd languished after most of your life. All right, so he isn't your brother technically. And as you explained, he knew nothing of your feelings for him. But at that moment in time it was obvious to the blindest of observers that Marcus Lawrence had discovered feelings he didn't know he had and they were nothing to do with fraternity. So I just backed off and left the field to him. I believed that was all you'd ever wanted, remember.'

'Oh, I see,' said Chloe, in a flat voice. 'You thought that Marcus would give Lisa the push and ride off with me into the sunset.'

'You said nothing in your letter to make me believe differently,' he pointed out grimly.

Chloe subsided against her pillows, her eyes bleak. 'No. It never occurred to me. I thought it was obvious, that you'd seen——'

'Seen what?' he said swiftly.

She looked down at her sore hands. 'That I wasn't a willing partner to the embrace, that I was trying to escape to get back to you.'

Piers sat down on the edge of the bed. 'All I saw was you two together. It's all I've been able to see ever since, indelibly printed on my mind.'

She breathed in deeply, not looking at him. 'He was eight, you see, when our parents got married. And he went away to school almost at once, so all my life I've only seen Marcus in snatches. School holidays, university vacations and so on. He was a god-like being who provided the excitement in my life. I suppose my first adult feelings for him came with all the usual hormone changes of puberty. From the time I was thirteen my friends sighed over actors and rock stars, but I had Marcus. He was the sole object of my hero-worship, while to him I was just the little nuisance who trailed round after him. It was a terrible fight, sometimes, to keep my feelings secret, though until recently I genuinely believed I had. The real watershed in my life was my start in modelling.'

'And suddenly the butterfly emerged from the chrysalis,' said Piers expressionlessly. 'It's obvious now why he was in such a rage with young Armstrong that morning.'

'But you do realise that he still didn't know why. It took you to open his eyes completely,' said Chloe, clearing her throat.

'When, exactly?'

'The Sunday before the wedding.' She raised dark-ringed eyes to his. 'To quote Marcus, you couldn't keep your hands off me—his words, not mine.'

'He was right,' said Piers huskily, holding her gaze.

'But what was worse, from his point of view,' she went on with difficulty, 'he realised I felt the same about you. Only a lot more than mere physical attraction. Marcus sensed I loved you before I knew myself.' At the sudden leap of fire in his eyes she bit hard on her trembling lower lip, and Piers took her sore hand in his and squeezed it convulsively.

Chloe let out a cry of anguish, tears pouring suddenly down her face, at which point Lisa knocked and put her head round the door to see if either of them would like something to eat.

'No! No, thanks,' gasped Chloe, sniffing hard. 'But perhaps Piers would like something.'

'No I would not,' roared Piers, giving Lisa a look which sent her running back downstairs at top speed. He swore under his breath, eyeing Chloe ruefully. 'And now, I suppose, Marcus will come charging up here to break my jaw for making you cry.'

Chloe groaned, then stiffened as footsteps sounded on the stairs, right on cue. She held up her arms in entreaty. 'Quick. Kiss me—*please*!'

Piers sat on the bed and pulled her into his arms with alacrity, obeying her command with such impassioned intensity neither of them saw the man who stopped dead in the doorway until Marcus coughed and made his presence known.

'Sorry to interrupt,' he said gruffly, 'but Lisa said Chloe was crying. Are you in pain? Is there anything I can do?'

Chloe smiled, and shook her head, secure in the embrace of arms which tightened possessively about her.

'It was my fault,' said Piers evenly. 'I hurt her hand.'

Marcus gave him a belligerent look. 'Just make sure that's all you hurt from now on.'

'You have my word on that,' returned Piers emphatically, then smiled. 'It won't surprise you to hear I intend to marry your sister as soon as it can possibly be arranged. If she agrees, will you give her away?'

Chloe held her breath, not only at hearing Piers's plans, but because it was obvious Marcus had registered the emphasis on the word 'sister'. He stared into Piers's eyes for a moment, then nodded, smiling wryly.

'You'd better not give the job to someone else! Of course I'll do it.' His eyes softened as he looked at Chloe. 'Gwen thinks you should both have something to eat.'

'We will soon,' Chloe promised him, her relief so intense that she sagged in Piers's arms as she realised a truce had been declared by the two most important men in her life.

'I'll make sure they all leave you both in peace until Piers says the word,' promised Marcus. He moved nearer and brushed a hand over Chloe's hair. 'See you later.'

When they were alone Chloe clutched Piers in relief. 'Please hold me close—even closer than that. Convince me I'm safe.' She burrowed against him convulsively. 'I was so *afraid*—such a coward, Piers.'

'Coward!' He tipped her face up to his. 'You engineer your own escape, stagger miles to get help, and still call yourself a coward?'

'I was sure he'd kill me once you wouldn't pay the money to get me back, you see,' she explained shakily.

'What on earth are you talking about?' he demanded, astonished. 'I'd have paid anything the man asked.'

Chloe's eyes filled with tears again. 'Would you? Would you really?'

'Darling, I love you so much the man could have taken everything I possessed as long as he gave you back to me,' said Piers in a voice which made Chloe's tears flow even faster.

'I thought you didn't believe in—in that kind of thing,' she gulped thickly, and waved a hand towards her dressing-table. 'There's a box of tissues over there.'

'I hope it's full,' said Piers, some of his normal assurance returning. 'If you keep on weeping at this rate I'll have to send down for reinforcements.'

'Sorry to be such a watering pot. It's reaction, I suppose.' Chloe mopped herself up determinedly. 'And to be honest part of it's relief because you and Marcus aren't at daggers drawn any more. I'm still very fond of him, you know.'

'I suppose I can live with that.' Piers kissed her quivering mouth. 'But I'm more interested in the way you feel about me.'

'I can give you the exact moment when the truth hit me in the face,' she said, with a shuddering sigh. 'When Marcus went mad and tried to kiss me my world turned upside down. Up to then he'd been out of reach on his pedestal, then suddenly he came crashing down from it complete with feet of clay and I hated it. Then I saw you looking at me with that terrible disgust in your eyes and I realised it was you I'd loved from the first, only I was too stupid to know it.' Something occurred to her. 'By the way, how do you happen to be here tonight? Didn't Ronald Hicks want the money quickly?'

'He knew I couldn't get such a big amount until Monday. And my aunt's legacy was my best bet at such short notice; it's deposited here, ready to use for Clieve House. Since his next communication was to be Monday evening, with instructions on where to make the drop, I drove straight here, to be with your family until I could contact the bank.' His face settled into grim lines. 'Hicks should be getting back to Fleck's Farm shortly, to a warm reception from the police.'

'He might have intended leaving me on my own the whole weekend.'

'I said I'd need something else of yours before I'd part with any money, so he was forced to go back.'

Chloe gave a great shudder, and Piers stretched himself out on the bed beside her and took her in his arms very carefully, mindful of her bruises. 'Let's forget about Hicks. Let me just hold you like this for a while, then I'll go down and tell your family we're going to be married as soon as I can arrange it. And no dashing off to a furtive little ceremony on our own. I want the whole works, with you in a stunning white dress and organ music and flowers, and everyone we know to be there to wish us well, your Mrs Taylor included.'

Chloe smiled at him incandescently. 'I'll be honest, Piers, it's what I've always wanted, too, but I suggested something quiet before to avoid being given away by Marcus.'

'Since I've already dealt with that, let's get on with the rest of the arrangements. From now on I want you where I can keep an eye on you at all times.'

'Then you'd better get me a job in your chambers,' she said pertly, luxuriating in the security of his embrace.

'And have young Chandler and lord knows who else hanging round you! Certainly not,' he said with finality. 'Think again, Chloe Lawrence.'

'Surely you don't expect me to sit at home and twiddle my thumbs?'

'No. You can find some other work in London, if that's what you really want—as long as it's not in my chambers.' He smiled slowly, his eyes close to hers. 'I work better without distractions.' He felt in his pocket and produced a box. 'Now you can have the ring back.'

Chloe sighed regretfully. 'Only I can't wear it yet. My fingers are swollen.'

'Then hang it on a chain round your neck,' he ordered, and grinned as her stomach gave a very unromantic grumble. 'You must be starving. So am I. I haven't been eating very well lately.'

'That makes two of us.'

They looked into each other's eyes for a long moment, then Piers kissed her very deliberately, commitment in the caress rather than passion. 'No more secrets I should know?' he asked sternly.

Chloe's eyes dropped. 'No. What you see is what you get.'

He groaned suddenly, burying his face in the pillow beside her. 'I just wish that were true right now. I'd like to whisk you off to my place this very minute and shut the rest of the world out until we'd got over all this trauma.'

'Instead of which,' said Chloe, pushing him away gently, 'you are going to go downstairs and ask for some food for both of us, and when we've eaten it we invite everyone up here to ask the questions they must be dying to ask. I'd much rather be alone with you, but that's what we'll do just the same, because that's what being part of a family entails, Piers Audley. Are you sure you want to marry into mine?'

Piers slid to his feet, smiling ruefully. 'Since it's the only way I can get you I don't have much choice, do I?' He turned in the doorway. 'By the way, I should warn you that instead of putting the police on Ronnie Hicks's trail we had the devil's own job stopping Marcus from staking himself out at Fleck's Farm so he could catch the man himself and teach him a lesson, to use his own words. By which I assume Marcus meant to thump the living daylights out of the man stupid enough to kidnap you.'

Chloe stared at him, horrified. 'I suppose Mother soon put a stop to that!'

'There was a loud outcry of general protest,' said Piers drily, 'but it was Lisa who made him see sense. Apparently she felt Daddy would take a dim view of his junior partner getting embroiled in anything so unsuitable. I didn't know "Daddy" was Marcus's senior partner in the practice, by the way. I thought there must be more to Lisa's attractions than met the eye!'

Chloe wagged a disapproving finger at him. 'At least she managed to rid Marcus of such a stupid idea. For a doctor Marcus does rather tend to use his fists too much on occasion.'

'Only where you're concerned, as Jessica pointed out to him tonight,' Piers informed her drily. 'From now on he'll just have to come to terms with the fact that you've got all the protection you can handle. Mine!'

'Very masterful!' Chloe's eyes narrowed challengingly. 'Which reminds me. If you really are in love with me——'

'Which I am,' he said with emphasis. 'I love you in every way possible, Chloe. More than I thought I could love anyone.'

'I wish I'd known!' she said, secretly ecstatic at his admission. 'How long has it been going on?'

'The moment I saw you coming down those stairs towards me.' He smiled wryly. 'Hackneyed, isn't it? I fell in love at first sight.'

'Then why all the smoke-screen about being incapable of it?'

'I had to cure you of this phantom love of yours before I let you know how I really felt,' said Piers, shrugging.

His eyes gleamed. 'Besides, much as you attracted me, at first I disapproved of you a little.'

'Why?' she demanded indignantly.

'I thought you'd dropped out, resigned from the real world to hide down here, safe with your mother.'

'So I only received the Audley seal of approval after you discovered I was a respectable working girl,' she retorted, eyes flashing.

Piers came back to the bed and sat down on the edge of it so their eyes were on level. 'Not true. I admit I disapproved of what I saw as a decision to run home to your ivory tower, but right from the first I was hell bent on luring you out of it.'

'Why?' said Chloe, knowing the answer, but wanting to hear it just the same.

Piers leaned forward and kissed her hard. 'So you could live happily ever after in the real world—with me.'

A few weeks later, just as long as it took for the bride's bruises to fade, the church at Little Compton celebrated the second Lawrence wedding of the year. It was no less festive than the first, though this time a longer guest list necessitated a marquee on the Parsonage lawn for the reception. In glad compliance with her groom's request, the bride wore an exquisite dress in unadorned ivory silk, complete with train and long floating veil secured with a coronet of ivy leaves and rosebuds. Her only jewellery, as described in the local paper the following week, was a pair of magnificent earrings in the shape of crystal hearts pendant from sapphire clusters, a present from the groom.

'Such a pity,' said Louise Dawson to the bride's mother at the reception, 'that Marcus's wedding couldn't be in Little Compton too, then you'd have had a hat trick, Gwen.'

Gwen Lawrence looked at her radiant daughter laughing up into the possessive, gleaming eyes of her new husband, and drank some champagne in glad, private toast. 'I'm perfectly happy the way things are, Louise, believe me.'

When the Audleys got back from a very protracted honeymoon one of their first social engagements, after a trip to see Gwen, was with the Warrens, a happy, relaxed evening spent in leisurely conversation round the dining table their hosts had just bought for their newly renovated house in Ealing.

'Marriage suits you both,' commented Jess as she refilled their coffee cups. 'You look positively blooming, Chloe.'

Piers eyed his wife with smug, triumphant pleasure. 'She certainly does.'

David Warren passed him the port decanter. 'Funny really. It's not so long since Chloe took no apparent interest in men at all, yet now here you are, an old married couple all in the space of a few months. Was it love at first sight?'

Chloe exchanged a look with her husband.

'It was for me,' said Piers, holding the look. 'I was knocked for six by the vision that came floating down the Parsonage staircase on New Year's Eve.'

'Remembering the situation David discovered you in later that night, I can well believe it!' said Jessica, chuckling.

'More like Christmas than New Year's Eve, to find Chloe in your room,' commented David.

'It was an eventful occasion all round,' agreed Piers. 'Though not one that fool Armstrong must look back on with pleasure.'

'He's finished his year's training at Marcus's practise, to his relief,' said Jess. 'I gather relations between them were rather strained after the party. Talking of Marcus, Chlo, have you bought something new for the wedding of the year?'

'Hobson's choice,' said Chloe enigmatically, her eyes dancing as they met her husband's.

Piers grinned. 'She means not only new but a bigger size.'

Jess stared from one triumphant face to the other then sprang to her feet and rushed to hug Chloe. 'No wonder you're blooming—you're pregnant! Does Gwen know? Have you told Marcus?'

Piers took his wife's hand. 'Gwen yes, Marcus no. You two were next on the list.'

As they lay in bed together that night, Chloe raised herself on one elbow to look down into her husband's face. 'Remember what you said about secrets, Piers?'

'Yes.'

'I fibbed.'

His eyes narrowed. 'You mean there's still something in your past I don't know?'

'Not in my past exactly. This dates from knowing you. Very much so,' she added.

Piers sat up and thrust the pillows behind him in the way she'd come to know so well. He held out his arms. 'Come here and tell me what you're talking about. I notice you chose your moment carefully, by the way.'

'What do you mean?' she said demurely, curling up against him.

'You wait until I'm replete with your sister's excellent dinner, and mellow with David's equally excellent port, then when we get home you seduce me——'

'And a lot of seducing it took, didn't it!' she retorted.

'That's irrelevant. I repeat, you seduce me until I'm vulnerable and helpless——'

'Piers Audley, vulnerable and helpless? That'll be the day.'

He looked down into her face, suddenly serious. 'So what's all this about a secret?'

Chloe smiled cajolingly. 'It's to do with the baby's birthday.'

A flash of alarm lit his eyes. 'You said everything was fine when you saw the consultant today.'

She nodded, pushing the bright hair back from her face. 'It is. But I'm afraid young Audley is likely to arrive earlier than our marriage lines indicate.'

Piers stared at her for a long moment, then slid his hands into her hair, holding her head still as he gazed down into her face. 'You mean he owes his existence to the first time we spent the night together here?'

'Afraid so.'

He frowned. 'But didn't you know?'

Chloe's lids dropped to hide her eyes. 'Of course I knew.'

'Is that why you tried so hard to contact me?'

Her lids flew up. 'Certainly not!' she snapped, eyes blazing, then bit her lip. 'I thought I'd put paid to his chances when I did my Houdini act from Fleck's Farm, but he's obviously a fighter. He hung in there.'

Piers crushed her close. 'Why didn't you tell me?'

'I wanted you to marry me for different reasons,' she said defensively. 'Not because you felt obliged to. Do you mind, Piers? Are you angry with me, will you be embarrassed?'

'No, no and no,' he said, kissing her. He held her away. 'In fact it's rather ego-boosting.'

'Because you hit gold first time?' she said, giggling.

'I'd have preferred a more elegant way of putting it, but yes, that's it exactly.' He shivered, sliding down with her beneath the covers. 'I'm bloody glad I didn't know all this when you were kidnapped. It was bad enough as it was.'

'When I fell the last few feet on my climb down the farm wall it was all I could think of as I lay on the ground trying to pull myself together,' Chloe said, heaving a sigh. 'I was terrified I'd lose the baby.'

His arms tightened. 'But we were still at loggerheads at that point. As far as you knew I was still refusing to have anything to do with you.'

'It made no difference. With you or without you, I still wanted my child.'

'Mine too!'

'Ours, then.' She surrendered ardently to his kiss. 'There. That was my last and quite nicest secret. Nicer than the other one, anyway.'

'Very true. Though if you knew earlier why did you wait until now to tell me? I suppose you wanted me helpless under your spell!'

'And are you?'

'Helpless?' He breathed in sharply at the touch of her hands. 'Utterly!' He turned her over and kissed her hungrily. 'I wish I'd met you years ago,' he muttered against her mouth.

'So do I.'

'Even though you were always languishing after Marcus?'

'Once I knew you, I stopped,' she reminded him, then her eyes narrowed as she saw his smile. 'Why so smug?'

Piers smoothed her hair, his eyes gleaming under his lowered lids. 'I was thinking how much I'll enjoy telling Marcus our news.'

'Let's not talk about Marcus,' said Chloe quickly.

'Divert me, then.'

'How?'

'In the way you learned so quickly it's hard for me to believe you were unversed in such things until so recently!'

'I would have thought you'd be pleased. After all, you were my instructor, Piers Audley!'

His eyes met hers with the look which always took her breath away. 'Pleased, Chloe Audley? The rest of my life won't be long enough to marvel at my good fortune.'

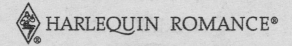

HARLEQUIN ROMANCE®

brings you

More Romances Celebrating Love, Families and Children!

We have a wonderful book for you in April in
our Kids & Kisses series—**Bachelor's Family**,
Harlequin Romance #3356, by the ever-popular
Jessica Steele. Fabienne Preston and Vere Tolladine
seem intent on misunderstanding each other until the
two adorable seven-year-old twins, Kitty and John,
play their part in the unfolding romance and make
their dream of being together a reality!

and coming in May...

Harlequin Romance #3362
The Baby Business
by Rebecca Winters

HARLEQUIN®

PRESENTS
RELUCTANT BRIDEGROOMS

Two beautiful brides, two unforgettable romances...
two men running for their lives....

My Lady Love, by Paula Marshall, introduces
Charles, Viscount Halstead, who lost his memory
and found himself employed as a stableboy by the
untouchable Nell Tallboys, Countess Malplaquet.
But Nell didn't consider Charles untouchable—
not at all!

Darling Amazon, by Sylvia Andrew, is the story of
a spurious engagement between Julia Marchant
and Hugo, marquess of Rostherne—an engagement
that gets out of hand and just may lead Hugo to
the altar after all!

Enjoy two madcap Regency weddings this May,
wherever Harlequin books are sold.

REG5

HARLEQUIN ROMANCE®

brings you

When you read **Invitation to Love** by Leigh Michaels,
you will know there are some wonderful reading hours
ahead of you with our **SEALED WITH A KISS** titles!

In April we have chosen **Dearest Love,** by Betty Neels,
Harlequin Romance #3355, all about sensible
Arabelle Lorimer and the rich and handsome
Dr. Titus Tavener, who both seem to be agreed on
one thing—that they make a very suitable couple.
But what happens when love unexpectedly
enters the picture?

Look out for the next two titles:

Harlequin Romance #3361
Mail Order Bridegroom
by Day Leclaire in May

Harlequin Romance #3366
P.S. I Love You
by Valerie Parv in June

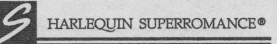